'What do you c

demanded.

'Because,' he bit out

again, impaling her with their molten intensity, 'I let no man take what's mine.'

'I am not yours!'

'But you will be,' Reid threatened, 'before this is over... but not now.' Abruptly, he released her, moving away from the fire, shoving his hands deep in his pockets. 'Relax, Kath; you're safe for tonight. I don't take another man's leavings.'

Dear Reader

Who are your favourite Mills & Boon heroes? We'll bet our bottom *ecu* that European men—French, Greek and Italian—will be among them. There's something unique about courtship Continental-style! Which is why Mills & Boon has launched *Euromance*—a book each month that features a gorgeous hero from one of the twelve EC countries. This month you can experience the sensual charm of the Irish, in Emma Richmond's gentle tale, LOVE OF MY HEART—look out for the attractive paperback cover!

The Editor

Elizabeth Barnes lives with her husband and son near Boston, Massachusetts, and vintage cars are a long-standing passion of the whole family. In fact, she decided her husband-to-be must be serious when he taught her to drive his 1904 Franklin—which has now figured in one of her books. In addition to vintage cars, she likes to see all treasures of the past preserved, and was involved in the restoration of a local nineteenth-century church after it was badly damaged by fire.

FORGIVE AND FORGET

BY

ELIZABETH BARNES

M I L L S & B O O N L I M I T E D
ETON HOUSE 18-24 PARADISE ROAD
RICHMOND SURREY TW9 1SR

First published in Great Britain 1993
by Mills & Boon Limited

This edition 1993

ISBN 0 263 78012 0

Set in Times Roman 10 on 10½ pt.
01-9305-60069 C

Made and printed in Great Britain

CHAPTER ONE

WHEN the phone rang, Kathy grabbed for the whistling kettle, and splashed boiling water on the granules of instant coffee in her mug. Unfair! she thought; no one should call this early—not yet eight, and on a Saturday, for pity's sake! It didn't help that the spartan little kitchen was bright with sunlight reflecting off the snow; for Kathy, the sun didn't shine—or shone unnoticed—until she'd had some coffee. Now, as the phone rang a second time, she risked a quick sip, predictably burning her tongue.

Malcolm, she told herself on the third ring. It was bound to be Malcolm, the original early morning man, the workaholic, non-respecter of other people's days off—Malcolm, with some minor point to be checked, and no matter that the library didn't open until ten.

She reached for the phone, cutting the third ring in half, tucking the receiver between her ear and her shoulder. 'Yes! Hello,' she said crossly, and waited for Malcolm's deep tones and precise phrasing.

Instead, there was a pause, then a whisper of a voice, thin, cracked and faded—like an old newspaper exposed too long to the light, then crumpled. 'Kathy, my dear, I'm so glad I caught you!' Then came a pause, before the voice continued more doubtfully, 'This is Kathy, isn't it?'

'Yes.' Kathy had been so sure it would be Malcolm; now she was forced to shift gears. 'Aunt Margaret?' It must be—no one else she knew sounded so time-worn and fragile—but Aunt Margaret never called. She wrote gentle, rambling letters: spidery script on ecru bond, the faint scent of lavender clinging to the sheets. 'Is something wrong?'

'It's my church, in Vermont. I'm up here for Christmas, and there was a fire yesterday... The church burned—not to the ground, but it's terribly damaged. There's all that charred wood, and the smell...' Aunt Margaret's voice wavered briefly; she drew a deep breath. 'Well, it's quite awful,' she continued more firmly, 'and such a to-do about it! Reporters and photographers all over the place, standing around, asking questions and taking pictures—as though this was an event we'd put on just for them... Dear, do you take a morning paper?'

'Yes.' After she'd put the kettle on to boil, Kathy had retrieved the paper from the front step; still folded, it lay on the counter next to the stove. 'Why?'

'There might be a picture. We've been told that our poor old church made the front pages all over the country. What with everyone printing in colour these days, and with the church being really quite lovely—a typical old New England church and all that... Well, it appears that we've been the answer to a great many editors' prayers—if such people do pray, which I doubt...

'We've been told that today is a slow day for news,' Aunt Margaret continued while Kathy grabbed for her paper, stretching the telephone cord nearly to breaking point in the process. 'A slow weekend, actually,' Aunt Margaret corrected. 'They say nothing happens the weekend between Christmas and New Year's Eve, which is why——'

'Yes, it's here,' Kathy interrupted as she unfolded the paper. 'On the front page.'

'Then you see...'

Kathy saw. For a newspaper picture, it was remarkably clear, showing her the classic lines of the old white church, the wreaths and garlands decorating the entrance, the slender spire against a clear blue sky. The picture could almost have passed for a Christmas card, except for the dark smudges of smoke around the spire and the flames—brilliant crimson and yellow. Plenty of colour, Kathy noted; enough colour to enliven even the dullest front page. 'Yes, it's here.'

'Then you can tell that it's a fine church, and I thought...' Aunt Margaret broke off for an instant, then continued with greater purpose in her frail, ancient voice, 'You see, some people have already decided that it ought to be torn down... which is why I called you.'

'For advice?' Kathy asked carefully, feeling her way. 'Did you want——'

'—you to come up,' Aunt Margaret finished for her, pre-empting any lesser alternative Kathy might have offered. 'I thought you might have time—what's left of the weekend, if you have nothing else planned, and perhaps another day or so... Could you come up and take a look? You would know what we've got—after all, it's your speciality, isn't it?—and if it's worth saving. You'd stay with me, of course, and we could have a nice visit. You've never been up here,' she added, coaxing, 'and I've wished you could come... Won't you, please? It would mean so much...'

'But...' Kathy paused, thinking hard. In the past, they'd met only on neutral ground in New York. She'd never even visited Aunt Margaret's apartment on Fifth Avenue, much less been a house guest... But this wasn't New York, Kathy reminded herself. How could there be any harm—or any danger—in staying with Aunt Margaret in Vermont? 'It's just... I wouldn't want there to be——'

'Any embarrassment?' Aunt Margaret suggested. 'My dear, there's no chance of that—none at all! I understand perfectly how you feel, although I always have thought it was a pity... but that's neither here nor there! No, you needn't worry. There will be no chance—I live very quietly here, and I've told no one about—well, the whole business. It would be just the two of us, and Emma, of course—my housekeeper. Do say you'll come! It would mean so much to have your thoughts on our poor church...' By the end, Aunt Margaret's voice was wavering; she had to stop and draw another deep breath before she could continue.

'I was married in that church,' she explained apologetically. 'I can see it from my front windows, just across the green. It's always been such a part of my life here, and I should hate to have it torn down if there's a chance... It's almost divine intervention—don't you think?—that this should happen, when it's what you know best. Please say you'll come!'

She really hadn't had any choice, Kathy acknowledged after she'd scribbled down Aunt Margaret's vague directions and hung up the phone. To have ignored that gentle plea would have been unthinkable! Kathy owed the older woman too much, a debt of gratitude which went way back. Aunt Margaret had been there for Kathy when no one else had cared at all; of course she could spare a few days, so long as there was—how had Aunt Margaret put it?—no chance of embarrassment. A fine euphemism, Kathy reflected, smiling faintly. Without actually giving anything away, 'embarrassment' covered a lot of ground—not that 'embarrassment' was the word Kathy would have chosen to describe how she'd feel if——

'I don't believe I'm up this early...and on a Saturday.'

The grumble, complete with Texas drawl, broke into Kathy's thoughts; she glanced up at Luce—the latest in a long line of student tenants. When Kathy had first signed the lease on the apartment, finding someone to share the expenses had been a necessity. Back then, she'd still been struggling to pay her debts; now, with the loans repaid, she still clung to the habit of frugality. Sharing expenses made sense, and the apartment was large enough—large living-room, two small bedrooms, a tiny bath and a kitchen big enough to accommodate a table and four chairs. Besides, sharing was handy whenever business took her out of town for a few days—someone in residence to feed the cat and water the plants. Then too, sharing the apartment also cut the loneliness—not that Kathy often acknowledged that, even to herself. She preferred to think of herself as completely independent; to admit to loneliness would be to admit that the life she'd carefully constructed was something less than perfect—and that she would not do.

For the most part, Kathy found her flatmates through the housing offices of Brown University or the Rhode Island School of Design, both nearby. Except for Carla, who'd been addicted to heavy metal rock music, played at full blast, Kathy had been fortunate in her choice of students. Luce, though, was proving to be the most satisfactory; even after just a month, she had proved to be good company, a pleasure to have around.

Now Luce checked the kettle, decided the water was marginally hot enough, and fixed herself a mug of instant coffee. 'That must have been Malcolm,' she observed, sitting down opposite Kathy at the kitchen table. 'No one else would call at such an ungodly hour.'

'I thought so too,' Kathy allowed with a faint smile. Normally, she was too loyal to permit criticism of Malcolm. He wasn't just her employer; he was—for lack of any better way to describe their casually close relationship—her good friend. He'd also encouraged her to advance herself, had given her opportunities to assume more responsibility in her work for him. She had plenty of reasons to be grateful to him, enough to put down anyone who dared to criticise him, but—well, Luce was different. In her considered opinion, Malcolm was entirely too single-minded, but she was outspoken without being mean, and there was always a bright edge of humour behind her words—humour, and more than a little truth.

'You're wrong,' Kathy said now. 'This time it wasn't Malcolm.

'Then who?'

'Aunt Margaret.'

'You've got an Aunt Margaret?' Luce enquired, cocking her head to one side. 'I thought you said you didn't have any relatives.'

'She's not really my aunt,' Kathy explained. Explanations, the retelling of the same personal details, was the price she paid for having a succession of flatmates. 'That's just what everybody calls her. We met...' She stopped to censor herself. Luce knew the bare outline—how Kathy had grown up in the Caribbean, that she'd first come to the United States when she was eighteen—but there was no need to go into precisely how and why she and Aunt Margaret had met! 'We met when I first came to New York,' Kathy continued, hoping Luce hadn't noticed the slight hesitation. 'She's a dear, close to ninety now. We keep in touch—we write, and I always see her when I'm in New York.'

'So why did she call before eight——' Luce smothered a yawn '—on a Saturday morning?'

'She's at her country place, and her church burned yesterday.' Kathy turned the newspaper around and slid it across the table to Luce, then started into the living-room to retrieve her road atlas. 'She wants me to come up for a few days, to take a look and decide if the building's worth saving.'

'And you're going?' Luce enquired, watching curiously as Kathy returned to the table to check the atlas. 'You're going to do it?'

'Mmm...I don't see why not,' Kathy agreed absently, studying maps, trying to find a logical route between Providence and the south-west corner of Vermont. 'Things are slow at the moment...'

'But still,' Luce persisted, 'you're going somewhere when it's not part of your job? Without planning everything days in advance? I don't believe it!'

The good-natured dig penetrated, and Kathy looked up. 'I am capable of some spontaneity,' she announced with dignity, knowing full well what was behind Luce's teasing.

The two of them were like night and day, almost impossibly different. While only three years younger, Luce made her feel old, Kathy thought with a sigh. Luce was an artist, her very real talent perfectly matched to a classic case of artistic temperament. She was incredibly vague about the practicalities of living, an impulsive free spirit who happily let circumstances dictate her decisions. Kathy, at twenty-six, was a creature of deliberate, sensible habit, intensely practical, someone who planned every move in advance—not that she'd always been like that, she reminded herself, sighing again.

For most of her first eighteen years, she'd lived a vagabond life, often depending on luck and the kindness of others to put food on the table and a roof over her head. She'd been a trusting soul—too naïve, she knew now—convinced that people were basically good, and that life always worked out for the best. Then it had all blown up in her face—the one time she'd made the mistake of letting someone get too close. It was a bitter experience, one which had changed her, made her everything that Luce wasn't—until today, when Aunt Margaret's frail little voice had lured her out of the safer pattern of her life.

'There's no reason why I shouldn't go,' Kathy explained now. 'Malcolm's away——'

'Which doesn't mean he won't call,' Luce pointed out drily, 'wanting you to do something for him in record time.'

'But it's not as though he demands that I sit home all weekend.'

'Not quite.'

'Besides,' Kathy continued, ignoring the dig, 'I *owe* Aunt Margaret!'

'I didn't think you owed anyone anything,' Luce observed, tilting her head to one side. 'I've never known anyone as independent as you are.'

'Well, I wasn't always,' Kathy retorted, and went back to her search for a logical route to East Hawley, finally concluding that there wasn't one. 'You'd think there would be a few roads on the diagonal,' she muttered disgustedly. 'I want to go north-west, and everything goes north or west, but not both. It's going to take me forever to get there.' She shut the atlas, the decided snap a sign of her frustration, then got up from the table. 'I'd better pack.'

'Need some help?' Luce asked, trailing after her down the narrow corridor which led to the bedrooms, matching actions to words when she reached down Kathy's suitcase from the high shelf in her cupboard. 'You're taking your usual uniforms, I suppose.'

'I don't see why not,' Kathy answered, plucking clothes from the cupboard—one pair of good wool trousers, one good wool skirt, one silk blouse and one cashmere sweater, one good wool dress which was slightly dressier then the rest, one good wool jacket which went with the conservative styles and muted colours of everything else. 'I don't like to bring too much with me, and these things work well together.'

'But it's all so predictable,' Luce protested, her own taste running to wild colours and outrageous styles, 'and so deadly dull.'

'I know,' Kathy agreed, adding two disreputable sweat-shirts and two pairs of faded jeans—work clothes—to the pile, 'but face it—I'm dull too.'

'Not really. At least...' as Kathy straightened up from her bureau drawers, arms full of underwear and tights, Luce paused thoughtfully '...you don't need to be,' she added as the two of them took a moment to study themselves in the mirror over the bureau.

Reflected back was an intriguing study in contrasts. Luce was tall for a girl—nearly five-ten—and slender almost to the point of being too thin, with dark eyes and short, curly black hair. Kathy, at least in her own opinion, was too short—not quite five-three—with definite curves in the right places. Her eyes were hazel, her hair a lightish blonde, shoulder length and almost straight, with only a slight curling up at the ends. 'You could make more of your hair,' Luce suggested hopefully, 'emphasise the colour... You'd look smashing in black or deep blue—true colours, not all those fuzzy blends.'

'It's a little late now to start making over my wardrobe.'

'It's never too late,' Luce objected, 'although it probably doesn't matter this time, with Aunt what's-her-name.'

'Margaret,' Kathy supplied, working quickly to fold clothes into the suitcase.

'Right. Aunt Margaret. So tell me——' Luce settled, cross-legged, on Kathy's bed '—when weren't you independent?'

'When wasn't I...?' Luce was a great one for doubling back on a conversation; it took Kathy a minute to catch the thread left hanging—in Luce's mind—in the kitchen. 'When I first came to New York. It was so cold, and I was so lonely...' But not at the very start, Kathy reflected, gripped by the intensity of her memories. What was wrong with her, for heaven's sake? She was remembering things she'd stopped thinking about years ago, and she couldn't blame that on Aunt Margaret. She'd seen the elderly woman any number of times without dredging up all this unwanted stuff—so why now? 'And Aunt Margaret was my only real friend for a while,' she finished briskly, shutting her suitcase and latching it closed.

'That's it. I'm on my way,' she announced, pausing only to jot down Aunt Margaret's address and telephone number. 'I'll be back Tuesday evening, but call if anything comes up—and don't forget the cat and the plants!'

Kathy drew a deep breath, her less than completely successful technique for conquering stage fright, then faced the group gathered to hear her conclusions. It had already been a long day, what with the drive up and the couple of hours she'd spent checking the outside appearance of the church. After that, she'd showered away the soot she'd collected, then shared a quick meal with Aunt Margaret and Emma. Now there was this meeting—the least favourite part of Kathy's work—to get through.

She waited while the movers and shakers of this small parish found themselves places to sit in Aunt Margaret's comfortable, faded living-room. The furnishings and decorations were an eclectic blend of antique and modern, and a cheerful fire burned on the hearth, its flickering flames casting interesting shadows, reflecting off each polished surface. It was all very civilised and serene, Kathy thought, wishing that such a calm setting would help her feel more relaxed.

'Well, perhaps we should start now,' Aunt Margaret said gently, her frail little voice instantly silencing the murmur of conversation. 'It's a happy coincidence that my young friend—Kathy Loring, for those of you who haven't been introduced—is a specialist in old churches. She's a member of the firm—Trowbridge Restorations—and well qualified to give us advice.'

'What we ought to do is tear it down, and everyone knows it,' a bluff, hearty middle-aged man stated firmly. 'Half of it's gone, and the other half's probably full of termites.'

Aunt Margaret murmured something suitably non-committal, looking across the room to appeal to the minister. 'Father Gardiner, before we start, would you offer a prayer?'

The prayer was dutifully offered, along with a few graceful remarks—thanking Aunt Margaret for her hospitality, and Kathy for making the trip to advise them. Then Father Gardiner subsided, and Kathy's time had come.

'What you have is a very nice church—at least it was very nice before the fire,' she qualified quickly. Malcolm wouldn't have told them that; he would have said that what they'd had before the fire was absolute rubbish—

second-rate Victorian attempts at Gothic, grafted on to a Type III New England church which might or might not have any merit.

That was Malcolm's technique—to hit people over the head with his sweeping pronouncements and superior knowledge. Malcolm never bothered with tact or explanations, which was why he hated to work on a church. Each church came with an untidy group of people, various committees, differing points of view. To work on a church took patience—never Malcolm's strongest suit. He much preferred private clients willing to leave all the decisions to him; once he'd realised that Kathy could pass for an expert on churches, he'd been happy to give all that work to her. She could be diplomatic, had the patience for endless explanations, and was willing to go slowly enough to build a consensus among her listeners—all qualities she could already see she would need with this group.

The middle-aged man, the one who had made the crack about termites, was clearly leading the charge to tear the church down and replace it with something cheaper and easier to maintain. He—what was his name? Kathy wondered, then it came to her: Mr Blunt—the aptly named Mr Blunt was going to be trouble, and Kathy was sure he wasn't the only one. There were others—at least three or four—watching her with sceptical, even doubting expressions. Only time would tell how easy they'd be to convince—and that was her job, she reminded herself, fighting a fresh flutter of nerves.

'I wasn't able to learn much today,' she explained now, trying to give herself courage by focusing on the facts, 'but even without going inside—which I wasn't able to do—I can be definite about a few things. First, the building appears to have been built between 1805 and——'

A brief murmur ran through the group—nothing to do with her, Kathy realised when she glanced up from her notes. There was someone at the front door—a latecomer to this informal meeting, she supposed. From where she stood, she had a partial view of the dimly lit entry hall, the front door wide open, Emma standing beside it to admit the new arrival.

He came through the doorway, nothing more than a dark shadow—a tall and lean shadow, Kathy noted. An important one, too, she decided, when Aunt Margaret got up from her chair and hurried into the entry hall. To have brought the meeting to a complete halt, this new arrival must have plenty of clout—more than Mr Blunt, Kathy mused. The living-room was now silent, people obviously straining to hear Aunt Margaret greet the stranger.

Kathy caught just a few words: 'Such a surprise... church burned yesterday.' But surely he already knew that, Kathy thought; why else had he come to the meeting? 'I hadn't expected...everyone here,' Aunt Margaret offered. 'Perhaps you'd prefer...'

'Don't see why...' the stranger said in response, the deep tones of his voice making his words as hard to follow as Aunt Margaret's '...see if I can help.'

'Good of you, if you're sure,' Aunt Margaret said, sounding very unsure of herself as she emerged from the shadowy hall to face the curious group in the living-room. 'This is such a surprise,' she announced, clearly flustered, her expression revealing a mix of emotions. 'He's been out of the country, travelling. He hadn't heard...my nephew,' she finally explained. 'I think some of you know him...'

Kathy shivered—a frigid draft of winter night air had made its way through the open front door, across the room to where she was standing.

'My nephew, Reid MacAllister,' Aunt Margaret said of the man who had moved into the room to stand beside her.

He was as tall and lean as his shadow, dark hair slanting across a high forehead, his features finely drawn, with deeply tanned skin taut over the strong bone-structure beneath, a firm mouth, nose slightly beakish—imperious was the word for it, Kathy told herself. He was dressed casually: light beige chinos which emphasised his long legs, a tweed jacket in shades of brown and beige, white dress shirt but no tie, the collar open—everything good quality, and worn with negligent ease. He had mature, seasoned good looks, Kathy thought, but there was an unyielding strength about him—something hard, an element of danger she could sense, if not define.

Aunt Margaret made introductions, saving Kathy for last. 'Kathy Loring,' she explained, 'a young friend of mine... She specialises in restoring old churches.'

'Does she?' the man enquired, subjecting Kathy to a careful inspection, absorbing the details—her blonde hair, her face, the simple lines of her cream silk blouse, the green wool jacket and blue-green wool skirt. 'How convenient.'

'Yes, I thought so,' Aunt Margaret agreed with surprising firmness. 'When I called her this morning, she was kind enough to agree to come up and share her expertise. She was just starting to explain what she was able to learn this afternoon——'

'When I interrupted,' he inserted smoothly. 'My apologies—Miss Loring, is it?' He inclined his head, his gaze holding hers for a long moment, then turned to take his seat in a wooden armchair by the fire. 'I won't hold things up any longer. Please continue, Miss Loring.'

As though he's in charge here, she noted, indignant. He even looked the part—a commanding presence in the armchair which suddenly—with him in it—appeared more like a throne. 'Thank you,' she managed through gritted teeth, glancing down at her notes, buying time while she put her feelings in order. 'I was explaining that the church was almost definitely built between 1805 and 1815.'

'As old as that?' Reid MacAllister asked with a sceptical lift of one eyebrow. 'I'd have guessed it was newer.'

So what do you care? It's not your church, Kathy thought, her gaze clashing with his. 'It looks newer because it was extensively renovated, probably before 1860. Tastes had changed by that time; people wanted their churches to be in the fashionable Gothic style.'

'What was done?'

'What's original, and what got added?'

'How can you tell if what we have is worth saving?'

Suddenly the questions were coming thick and fast; Reid MacAllister's had started the others—one reason to be grateful to him, Kathy conceded. She was equally grateful that he asked no more questions; she was more comfortable with the other people in the room—the ones who didn't watch her with such close attention, or with such a coolly speculative gaze.

'Then perhaps we do have something worth saving,' Father Gardiner summarised after more than two hours of hard questioning and discussion, 'but you'll want to go inside before you can be sure. How soon will that be, do you think?'

Kathy shrugged. 'Tomorrow, I hope, but the fire chief wants someone to decide if what's left is structurally sound before——'

'It's been years since that place was structurally sound,' Mr Blunt scoffed. He'd kept quiet longer than Kathy had expected, but now it was obvious that he'd had quite enough. In his mind, it was time to re-establish his dominance, to get back to the business of deciding to tear down what remained of the church. 'Anyone would be a fool to go back inside!'

'Well, perhaps, although we can't yet know for sure,' Father Gardiner murmured, playing peacemaker. 'What we need is some kind of an engineer—not easy to find on a weekend.'

'Would I do?' Reid MacAllister asked with an unreadable smile. 'It's what I do for a living, and I'd be happy to help, so long as Miss Loring is willing to trust my judgement.' It was meant to sound like a joke, but he was watching her even more closely now, willing her to respond. When she didn't, he pressed harder. 'Are you?'

'Of course,' she managed stiffly.

He smiled again, then leaned back in his chair, satisfied. 'Fine. I'll speak to the fire chief first thing in the morning, then check the place out. If it's safe, Miss Loring could spend most of the day at her sleuthing.'

'So it's settled,' Father Gardiner noted with pleasure, then offered a final brief prayer.

As soon as he'd finished, the room began to empty. People were clearly intent upon collecting their coats and getting home, pausing only long enough to say goodnight to Aunt Margaret, who stationed herself in the hall, by the front door. Kathy was left behind, alone in the room—except for Reid MacAllister. Uneasy, she turned away from his probing gaze, pretending to consult her notes.

'So,' he began, a hard edge to that one quiet word, 'What the devil are you doing here, Kath?'

CHAPTER TWO

'ISN'T that obvious?' Kathy asked in a furious whisper. After the ordeal of the meeting and his cat and mouse game—watching her, letting her wonder if he would say anything or not—it was almost a relief to turn and confront him. 'I'm here to help. Aunt Margaret asked me to come. What I want to know is what you're doing here!'

'Isn't that equally obvious?' Reid countered, a dangerous glint in his eye as he left his place by the fire and came towards her. 'I'm here for a visit.'

'She would have told me if you were coming.'

'She didn't know.'

'But...' Kathy stopped, because there really weren't any buts in this tangle. Reid was here—her worst nightmare made real—and she was helpless. This was Aunt Margaret's house; she was, after all, his real aunt—more precisely his great-aunt, his grandfather's sister. Kathy couldn't tell him to leave, which left her with only one way to safety. 'I'll leave,' she announced, 'first thing in the morning.'

'Well, you haven't changed in that respect, have you?' he observed, the hard edge back in his voice. 'But this time I'm not letting you off the hook. You're going to stay.'

'You can't tell me what to do,' she protested. 'Perhaps you've forgotten——'

'I haven't forgotten,' he informed her, moving closer, crowding her, forcing her back against the refectory table, 'but I wonder if you have.'

'Of course not,' she snapped, forced to look up now to meet his cold gaze—cold as ice, she thought, shivering; there was no warmth at all in his silvery eyes, but then, when had there ever been warmth? 'I'm not likely to forget what happened—which is why I'm leaving.'

'But this isn't the past,' he pointed out with a brief, meaningless smile. 'You're not going to let Maggie down, and you're going to make her believe that you can be civilised and adult about this. You'll do whatever it takes to keep her from being upset.

'Can't you see?' he persisted, correctly reading Kathy's stubborn expression. 'She's been failing, these last couple of years. Now even the small things upset her, and I'm not going to let you walk out on her.'

'You're not going to *let* me?'

'That's right, and believe me...' He paused, staring down at her, and she wondered how she'd made the mistake of thinking his eyes were like ice. Instead, they were blazing, molten silver, the only visible sign of towering anger only barely held in check. 'You won't like what will happen if you do anything—anything!—to upset her. Have you got that?'

Mutely, she nodded, refusing to give him the satisfaction of hearing her voice tremble she tried to speak.

'Good,' he said, holding her gaze a beat longer. 'I knew you'd see it my way.' He turned, then called back over his shoulder, 'Tell Maggie I've gone to my room.' He went out through the door which led towards the kitchen; a moment later Kathy heard him climbing the back stairs, just as the front door closed for the last time.

'Emma, don't bother with things tonight,' Aunt Margaret instructed as the two women stood together in the entry hall. 'You run home now, and clear away in the morning.' She waited until Emma was gone, then appeared in the living-room doorway to take a quick look around. 'Is Reid here?' she asked uncertainly.

'Gone up to his room,' Kathy explained, her voice carefully neutral. 'I think he was tired—I think we all are.'

'Yes, of course...' Aunt Margaret hesitated, then continued in a rush, 'My dear, I can't tell you how sorry

I am! I had no idea—he hadn't told me he was coming... Not that he ever does, but he was here so recently, just six weeks ago, and I never expected he'd be back so soon.'

'It's all right, really.' Kathy made herself smile. Reid told her that she must make Aunt Margaret believe that she could be civilised and adult about the situation, and the attempt had to start now. 'It's funny,' she began. 'You know that this is what I'd been dreading, but it really wasn't so bad. In fact,' she improvised boldly, 'I think it's for the best—to face him, and realise that the world won't come to an end. It was over between us eight years ago, and it's good to know that there's no anger left.'

'But to work with him—won't that be difficult?' Aunt Margaret probed gently. 'I'd certainly understand if you'd rather leave in the morning.'

Which was, of course, what Kathy most wanted to do—but couldn't, she knew. 'Don't be silly,' she said now, dropping a brief kiss on the parchment-pale cheek. 'Just think how lucky it is that he's here. Without his help, I might not get inside the church. Don't worry! Just go off to bed—this has been a long day for you, and everything's going to be fine.'

'Well, if you're sure,' Aunt Margaret agreed uncertainly—but wanting to be convinced, Kathy knew.

'Very sure,' she said firmly, pasting on another false smile, keeping it on until the older woman had disappeared into her bedroom—what had been the front parlour until the stairs had got to be too much for her to climb.

Finally alone, Kathy was in no mood to hurry upstairs to her room. Reid was upstairs; she'd give him first crack at the bathroom while she cleared away the cups and saucers and dessert plates.

When there was nothing left to be done, she still hesitated, loath to make a move towards the stairs. For pity's sake, why? she impatiently asked herself. She supposed she was worrying that Reid might ambush her at the top of the stairs—utter nonsense! she assured herself.

She was wrong. He was waiting for her, halfway down the shadowy upstairs hall, leaning against the wall beside her bedroom door, his arms crossed on his chest.

She stopped some distance away. 'What are you doing here?'

'Haven't we already been through that?' he enquired, sounding bored, as though speaking to an idiot child. 'You're here to help; I came for a visit.'

'That's not what I meant and you know it! What are you doing *here*—right by my bedroom door?'

'Nothing so terrible. I only wanted to tell you that I liked the way you handled things with Maggie. It was deftly done.'

'You were eavesdropping,' she accused.

'Listening,' he corrected carelessly. 'I wasn't sure I could trust you, or that I'd got my point across.'

'You had, although you ought to know me well enough to know that I'd never do anything to worry her.'

'But I don't know you—not at all,' he pointed out, all calm logic, in contrast to her anger. 'Never did, in fact, except to understand that you were a very clever girl...and you're even more so now. You've come a long way, Kath—quite the career woman, aren't you?'

'How would you know?'

'Because I've followed your progress—at a distance, of course,' he explained, and saw her eyes widen in shock. 'That's right, Kath. I've always made it my business to know where you were and what you were doing—although I have to admit that it didn't seem quite so impressive on paper. Seeing you in action tonight... Well, you're far more than a secretary in a small firm of restoration specialists. I was impressed.'

'Am I supposed to take that as a compliment?'

He shrugged. 'Take it any way you like. Let's just say that I found your performance enlightening. I can't wait for tomorrow.'

'Well, I can,' she snapped, warily circling his tall form to reach the door to her room, 'and now, if you don't mind——'

'Don't let me stop you,' he offered pleasantly. 'I'm not about to follow you, if that's what you're worried about.'

'I'm not worried!' She opened the door, making a point of not stepping into the room. 'Don't flatter yourself—nothing about you worries me.'

'No?' he asked, detaching himself from the wall, turning to face her. 'Then why, I wonder, did you tell Maggie that this is what you've been dreading?'

'Because it was true. I never wanted to see you again.'

'And now that you have?' he persisted. 'You told her that there was no anger left.'

'I lied. I had to, didn't I?' she pointed out as he took a step towards her, forcing her to stand her ground—the only alternative to retreating into her bedroom, where he could follow. 'You said I should make her think that I could be civilised about this.'

'So you are angry?'

'With you? Yes,' she spat out as he moved even closer and she had to lift her head to continue to meet his gaze. He was too tall, damn him! she fumed, remembering when she'd been thrilled by how tall he was, when his height had made him seem masterful, her powerful protector—what a fool she'd been! 'That's all I feel for you!'

'I wonder—as much anger as I feel for you?' he mused, staring down at her, studying—searching—her face. Then he smiled, that odd, unreadable smile that made her breath catch, caused her heart to skip a beat. 'Let's hope so,' he told her, 'because anger's the only thing that can get us through the next couple of days.'

He stepped back then, permitting her to close the door on him, permitting her to finally draw a breath.

He thought anger would get them through? Anger wasn't enough! she thought, dismayed to find that she was shaking. She wasn't sure anything would be enough;

she'd been right to dread the idea of having to face him again, and anger was only a small part of what she was feeling. All the rest was pain—that sense of betrayal she'd believed was safely buried, locked up with the rest of her memories...

She'd been told that she'd been born in the mainland United States; she had travelled on a US passport, but she'd been unable to remember any other life than one spent knocking around the Caribbean. At first—until she was about five—she'd travelled with both her parents. Then—in St Lucia, her father had told her—her mother had died. For the next five years, while Kathy's memories of the pretty blonde lady faded, she and her father had travelled alone—from one island to the next, wherever there was easy living and light work to be done.

On Martinique, when Kathy was ten, they'd met Paulette. She had dark hair and dark eyes; she was always laughing—as different from Kathy's mother as could be imagined, her father had told her, but Paulette had been his kindred spirit. She liked easy living as much, hard work as little as Kathy's father; they had made themselves into a family of sorts, the three of them travelling from one island to the next.

Kathy's father had died on Antigua, when she was fifteen; although Paulette had owed her nothing, she'd been willing enough to keep Kathy with her. The two of them had floated along until finally, just before Kathy's eighteenth birthday, they'd washed up on one of the very least of the Lesser Antilles. There Paulette had attached herself to a man who owned a quaint and charming old inn. Marrying Thom Vernick had been a step up for Paulette, giving her a more settled existence than she'd ever been able to achieve on her own, more settled than that she'd had with Kathy's father.

To Paulette's credit, she'd told Thom that Kathy would live with them; to his credit, he had agreed... but Kathy had soon recognised the writing on the wall. True, she'd done as much as she could to help—cleaning the guest rooms in the morning, waiting table at lunch and dinner—but the threesome was an uneasy arrangement. The inn was small, and Kathy had been painfully aware that her presence had a slightly inhibiting effect on Paulette and Thom. They'd never said a word, but it was obvious that they would have liked a little more privacy and time alone. Even worse, money had seemed always to be in short supply, and Kathy's room was one Thom would otherwise have rented to a tourist.

Still, their arrangement had continued its unsatisfactory course for a few weeks, until Kathy's eighteenth birthday, the day that Reid MacAllister appeared. Almost immediately the whole island knew that he was sailing alone, that he had put into the small harbour for provisions—and, he'd said, for a few hours of civilised existence. That meant the inn; he had checked in—taking the last guest room, excepting Kathy's—just before noon.

She had waited on him at lunch, had been dazzled by his worldly and dark good looks. He was nothing like the average tourists who flew in and out on the small plane which provided a twice-weekly service. He was—at least in Kathy's eyes—an adventurer, a man who sailed alone—'wherever the wind and currents take me', he'd explained. There were, of course, plenty of men like him sailing the Caribbean, but few of them put into this little backwater island. Kathy had never before met anyone like him—or if she had, she'd been too young to notice. Now, on her eighteenth birthday, she was suddenly thinking like a woman—and Reid MacAllister was a very attractive man. Too old for her, of course; she'd known that instantly, and the knowledge had made her painfully shy, even tongue-tied with him.

She'd hardly said three words to him as she'd served his lunch, might never really have spoken to him if he hadn't happened upon her small birthday celebration. Paulette and Thom had left it until mid-afternoon, a time when the guests were usually diving or on the inn's small crescent beach. Paulette had made a cake; the three of them had been alone on the shaded veranda, laughing as she tried to light all nineteen candles—'The last one is to grow on, *chérie*,' she'd explained, 'and you must make a wish and blow them all out—poof!'

I want to grow up! I want to find some way to leave the island, Kathy had wished passionately—and it was at that moment that Reid had come out on to the veranda. With a slight smile, he'd watched Kathy blow out her candles, and the gregarious Paulette had urged him to join them for the cake.

'If you're sure?' he asked with a lift of one eyebrow. 'I'm afraid I don't have a gift.'

'But you don't know me, didn't know it was my birthday,' Kathy protested, her cheeks lightly tinged with colour. 'Why should you have a gift?'

'Because an eighteenth birthday is special,' he answered with a heart-stopping smile. 'You're an adult now...' And something about the way he watched her, the spark kindling in his silver-grey eyes—unexpectedly light eyes for one with such dark hair and deeply tanned skin—made Kathy suddenly feel very adult.

He ate his cake, chatting idly with Thom and Paulette, even stayed while Kathy opened her two gifts—a pen and pencil set from Thom, an exotically patterned shawl from Paulette. 'Green and golden... it suits you,' he observed when Kathy wrapped herself in the emerald-green silk with its deep gold fringe and embroidered design. 'Youth,' he added with a rueful shake of his head, drifting away when some of the other guests returned from the beach.

Kathy served him again at dinner; he sat alone in a shadowy corner of the veranda, ignoring the tourists, their loud talk and occasionally raucous laughter. 'Was this afternoon the only celebrating you'll do for your birthday?' he asked when she brought the snifter of brandy he'd asked for with his coffee. 'Or will you go out partying when you're done here?'

'There's nowhere to party on the island,' she answered shyly, wondering... If there had been, would he have offered to take her out? 'At least—if people want to party, they come here.'

'And it's no fun, trying to party where you work,' he completed with another of those heart-stopping smiles. 'It doesn't seem fair.'

'Oh, I don't mind,' she assured him, forced to hurry away when one of the tourist parties hailed her.

By the time she had seen to their needs, Reid MacAllister had finished; his table was empty, and some of the magic seemed to have gone out of the night. Later, alone in her room and ready for bed, already wearing her white lawn nightgown, Kathy was unaccountably restless. An eighteenth birthday ought to be something different, something special, she thought, but hers had been special only when *he* had been there. And now? Now it was nearly midnight; her birthday was nearly over... Was this how it was going to end—with her alone in her room, fighting the siren call of the waves breaking on the small crescent beach?

Impulsively, she lifted the emerald and gold shawl from its box and draped it over her shoulders. Magic! she thought, letting herself out of her room, her bare feet silent as she went down the dark stairs and into the night. It was cooler outside, cool enough for the shawl to be more than an affectation, but on the deserted beach the fine sand still held some of the heat of the sun. She stood motionless, the wind off the water playing with her nightgown's long skirt, lifting her hair, causing the shawl to billow.

Magic! she thought again. It was magic to stand here like this, revelling in the sensuous stroke of the silk on her skin, magic to watch the waves touched with the cool light of the stars. Magic... and still her birthday... for a few minutes more.

'Still celebrating?' Reid MacAllister asked, amused, the sound of his voice placing him just behind her and off to the right.

'I—yes...' She turned towards him, her toes curling into the warm sand at the sight of his tall form, the light trousers and white shirt, the dark hair slanting across his high forehead, the strong planes and angles of his face. 'While I can.'

'And while I can——' he came closer, something laced through his fingers glittering in the darkness '—this is for you. Happy birthday.'

'Thank you.' She held out her hand, feeling no shyness, no fear—after all, this was part of the magic, she told herself as she felt the touch of cool metal on her palm. 'What is it?' she asked, holding it up, barely able to make out the gold links of the delicate chain and the small golden charms—a shell, a sand dollar, a seagull, a starfish, a sea-horse. 'It's lovely,' she breathed, 'but where did you find it?'

'In town, in one of the shops.'

'And bought it for me?'

'Of course. Don't sound so surprised.'

'But you hardly know me,' she pointed out, and he smiled.

'Does that matter? Any girl's eighteenth birthday should be special.'

'But mine already was, because you came,' she confessed candidly, then bit her lip, turning away from him to face the sea. Perhaps she'd been too honest, she worried. After all, he'd been talking about any girl—emphasis on the any, as in many. A man like Reid MacAllister would have known many girls—many women, she corrected. There was nothing boyish about him; he was a man—seasoned, mature. He'd have stopped paying attention to girls a long time ago, and he really wasn't paying attention to her—just being kind, she decided, closing her hand around the gold chain, one of the charms digging into her palm.

'Aren't you going to put it on?' he asked from behind.

She nodded, too self-conscious now to speak or even to face him. She needed both hands to slip the chain over her head; when she tried, the wind tugged at her shawl, threatening to snatch it away.

'Let me help,' he said, suddenly in front of her, taking the chain as she clutched at the billowing silk. 'May I do it?'

'Please.' She stared up at him, transfixed, as he lifted the chain over her head and it settled in place. She had never been this close to him—this close to any man for that matter, she realised, her breath catching when he started to work her hair free from the chain's confinement. Only a few inches separated them; he was so close that she caught the faint scent of his aftershave, cool and astringent, mingled with something more basic and elemental.

'Almost,' he said absently, and then nodded. 'There, that's it.' Briefly, his hand touched her nape—a small, insignificant movement, but to her a caress of delicate subtlety. She shivered and he glanced down, a quizzical expression in his silver eyes. 'Cold?'

'No,' she whispered against the racing beat of her heart. 'Not really.'

'Still, we ought to go in,' he decided, but he made no move to turn away. Instead, he bent his head; his lips—cool and restrained—briefly touched hers. 'Happy birthday,' he said, smiling, then straightened, putting a safer distance between them. 'I may not see you in the morning,' he continued after a moment. 'I plan to leave very early, with the tide.'

Her racing heart skipped a beat as the weight of depression settled within her. She didn't want him to leave, not so soon, not before she really knew him! If he would stay even a little bit longer, she'd have a chance... A chance! she thought, electrified. 'May I come with you?' she began in a rush. 'I'd work for my passage, and I wouldn't need to go far. Just to a bigger island—any one—would be fine. Perhaps Curaçao, or Trinidad? I don't know where you're going next, but that doesn't matter.'

'Doesn't it?' he asked, frowning. 'What would your parents think—or are you running away from home?'

'This isn't home—not really—and Paulette and Thom aren't my parents, so they wouldn't mind,' she assured him, then stopped, biting her lip when she saw his expression of disbelief. 'Please?' she coaxed. 'It's the perfect solution! They'd be relieved to have me go, and who knows when I'll have another chance? We're so out of the way here that not many boats come to the island, and most of those we do get don't want to take on a stranger, and of course I wouldn't go with just anyone... but I know I can trust you,' she finished triumphantly.

'Do you?' he asked with an odd, almost indulgent expression. 'I'm not sure you should.'

'Well, I am,' she stated—a flat declaration, no room for exceptions, 'and I'm an excellent judge of character. My father used to ask me—"Katie-bird, what do you say? Shall we go with these folks?" and we'd do what I said, and it always worked out for us. You see? I've been taking chances on people, knocking around this part of the world all my life. And I've never been wrong.'

'There's always a first time,' he reminded her.

'Not with you!'

'And what about your father?' he persisted, ignoring her last comment. 'Would he be coming too?'

'He died, three years ago,' she explained, her voice even, refusing to show him even a hint of emotion. 'I've been with Paulette since then, but now it's time for me to be on my own.'

'But taking a chance, when you're on your own, is a different proposition.'

'All the more reason to start with you,' she countered, so fiercely that he had to laugh.

'I'm flattered,' he observed drily, 'but I'd rather know why you want to leave. After all, this is a good little island...you've got a place here, and people who obviously care about you.'

'But it's too small,' she all but wailed, 'and there's no opportunity. I can't get ahead, can't *be* anything, if I stay here, and I don't have a place here—not really! I'm staying in one of Thom's guest rooms; if he didn't have me there, he could rent it, and I'm nothing to him, and not much more to Paulette... Poor Paulette! When she took me on, she didn't expect to have me underfoot for the rest of her life! Don't you see?'

'Afraid not,' he confessed with a smile. 'I might, though, if you told me the whole story.'

She did so, unemotionally and with spare economy, reciting the names of as many as she could remember of the islands she'd lived on, missing Reid MacAllister's shrewd gaze when she skimmed lightly over her father's death. 'So you see, it's not fair of me to stay around any longer. Paulette's never had as much security as she has now, with Thom. You must see that I can't ruin that!'

'I suppose I do,' he allowed grudgingly, 'but why choose me—why choose anyone? It would make more sense and be a whole lot safer if you flew off the island the next time the plane comes.'

'But that takes money, and I don't have any—at least not enough,' she explained; then, able to tell from his expression where his thoughts were going, she added emphatically, 'and I am not about to ask Thom for some!'

'Not even a loan?'

'No! He doesn't have much at the moment. Being married to Paulette costs him more, and because of me he's one room short on making expenses... Please?' she finished, and for the first time her voice wavered. 'I'd work—work just as hard as you want me to. I could crew——'

'I don't need a crew.'

'Then I could cook! I'm a really good cook. I'll cook you great meals, just until we get to some place where you can drop me off. I could clean, too, or polish the brass... Please?' she begged, taking his hands in both of hers. 'It would mean so much to me, and be such a small thing for you to do!'

'I'm not so sure about that,' he observed drily, gently withdrawing his hands, slipping them into his pockets. 'I think there might be more to your scheme than either of us can imagine.'

'But——'

'You'd better let me think about this,' he said, overriding her attempt to contradict him. 'You're very persuasive, but there might be——' he paused to choose his words carefully '—difficulties you haven't considered. In the morning—I'll be up at five. Ask me again in the morning.'

In the morning, he'd agreed to take her with him, but he shouldn't have, Kathy told herself now, lying tense and still wide awake between Aunt Margaret's lavender-scented sheets. The whole thing had been a terrible mistake. It had been the worst mistake of her life, and she was willing to bet—unfair as it might be of him—that Reid would say the same.

He'd been right, all those years ago. 'There might be difficulties,' he'd told her that night—the understatement of the century! Could the pain of betrayal be dismissed as a mere difficulty? she asked herself, her anger a palpable force in the darkness.

To have to face Reid again, after what he'd done to her! Kathy's hands curled, clenched into fists, her nails digging into her palms. Tomorrow, she thought, would be a horror, something she would have to endure—but only for Aunt Margaret's sake!

CHAPTER THREE

KATHY awoke to the heartening aroma of coffee—some compensation for a night of almost no sleep, she told herself as she hurriedly dressed in her work clothes of jeans and sweat-shirt. She tied her hair back with a red bandanna, then made her way down to the kitchen, blessing Emma for being an early riser. Then she froze on the threshold when she saw that Reid was alone in the kitchen.

'You're up early,' he observed, his voice empty of all expression. 'I thought I'd have the place to myself for a while.'

'And I thought Emma would be here.'

'Then we're both disappointed.' He turned his back on her to hunt through the refrigerator, producing a bowl of eggs and a slab of home-cured bacon. 'Should I include you?' he asked—a minimum pass at politeness—as he placed the food on the counter.

'No, thanks.' She advanced into the room—no sense trying to avoid the inevitable, she reflected. 'I'm not much for breakfast.'

'You never were,' he remembered with a sardonic smile, 'but help yourself to the coffee.'

Warily, she circled around him, found a mug, and filled it from the pot on the stove. 'I'd prefer,' she began carefully, retreating to the line of windows at the far end of the room, 'that you don't bring up the past.'

'Would you?' he asked, slicing bacon with a certain vengeance. 'Why? Do you like to pretend that it never happened?'

'Of course, but it's pretty hard to do.' Harder still today, she mused, when the past is just across the room, cooking breakfast. 'I just don't see the point in letting people here know that there was ever anything between us.'

'My aunt knows.'

'I'm well aware of that, but she assured me that no one else does.'

'Then how did she explain your sudden appearance on the scene?'

'That I'm a friend, someone she's known for years.'

'So our chequered past remains a deep dark secret?'

'Yes,' Kathy answered briefly, then bent her head to sip her coffee. Chequered past, she mused, such a convenient term. It was sufficiently vague, capable of hiding—of denying—a wealth of feelings, all the feelings which had once been alive between them. Trust Reid to come up with such a useful phrase! she reflected bitterly, feeling a little sick when the aroma of cooking bacon reached her. He was right: breakfast never had appealed to her, but it had been his favourite meal of the day—something she really had forgotten, disliked remembering now. 'I'll be in the library,' she announced, the words clipped and cool.

'Running away so soon, Kath?' he mocked, but she was already halfway across the room and chose not to respond.

There would be other battles to fight—ones worth fighting, she assured herself when she'd gained the sanctuary of the quiet, book-lined room. Besides, Aunt Margaret had said there were some town histories in here; they were bound to include something about the church, Kathy knew, even some photographs or drawings. She could keep herself occupied—keep out of Reid's way was a little more like it, she was forced to admit—for hours, until he was done with his breakfast, his meeting with the fire chief, and his inspection of the church. She might manage to have the whole morning to herself.

'Coming?' Reid asked peremptorily from the doorway.

'Now?' That much time couldn't have passed, Kathy assured herself, looking up from a history of East

Hawley. 'I'll wait until you've done your thing with the fire chief. There's no point in my going over now.'

'There is, if you know anything about how these churches are constructed,' he told her, a thread of impatience in his voice. 'I don't have a clue about old wooden buildings. I need your advice.'

There's something new, she thought, closing the history and getting to her feet. When, in the past, had Reid ever wanted—much less needed—her advice? 'All right,' she agreed meekly, resisting the urge to gloat. 'I'll do my best.'

'Just so long as we don't both break our necks...' He paused, fixing her with a piercing gaze. 'You do know what you're doing, don't you?'

'Of course,' she assured him pleasantly, collecting her jacket and the notebook she'd left on the chair. 'This is my field.'

'So you say.' He subjected her to a brief dark look, then led the way outside.

Aunt Margaret's house was on the small village green, almost directly opposite the fire-scarred church. Yesterday, when Kathy had made her first brief inspection of the building, she'd hurried across the green without a glance at her surroundings. Now, though, caught by the slanting rays of the rising sun, she felt compelled to pause on the granite doorstep to survey the scene which greeted her.

It was a glorious winter morning, this the perfect winter setting. Overhead, the sky was a deep, cloudless blue; the air was sharply cold, but beautifully clear and clean. Ahead, on the green, the bare skeletons of venerable maple trees dominated the view, creating a stark contrast to the harsh white of the snow and the softer white of the old colonial houses which ringed the green. There was a pleasing harmony, even symmetry, to the scene—so long as one avoided looking at the church, she acknowledged. Other than that, this world was breathtaking, exhilarating, absolutely perfect, she thought, busily absorbing impressions, recalled to the present only when she heard Reid call her name.

He had stopped at the end of the walk, had turned back to stare. 'Are you coming?' he demanded, impatient. 'What's the matter with you?'

'Nothing's the matter,' she told him, unable to suppress her smile. 'I'm just looking. I've never seen anything quite as lovely as this.'

'Try looking at the church,' he suggested pointedly. 'See how lovely that is.'

'Are you always this unpleasant?'

'It's the company,' he countered shortly, 'and I'd like to get this finished as soon as possible.'

'Well, the feeling's mutual,' she muttered, but there was no danger that he'd heard. He'd already started across the road which separated Aunt Margaret's house from the green. 'OK, Mr Sunshine, if that's how you want things to be,' she added, staring after him.

On a day as perfect as this one, she seemed to have left self-consciousness and anger behind. Well, now, perhaps that was going too far, she decided, enjoying the crunch of snow under her footsteps. She knew that somewhere, below this surface euphoria, she was still deeply angry, still profoundly conscious of the pain he'd once caused her. But never again, she vowed; he would never hurt her again. He couldn't, unless she let him get too close—and she was as likely to let that happen as he was likely to try!

Deliberately, she slowed her pace, ignoring Reid's tall figure and long strides while she studied the church. It was a dark and sullen presence in this pristine world. The white vinyl siding was now a dark, muddy grey, broken in places, melted in others. Windows were broken, some of the frames scorched black. One of the front doors had been wrenched off its hinges to lean at a drunken angle. Near the far left end of the building, the fire had broken through the roof to reveal the stark lines and angles of charred, broken rafters. Only the steeple appeared untouched, its narrow spire still pointing towards the brilliant sky, the steeple clock stopped at nine thirty-six.

By the time she'd completed her inspection, she'd nearly caught up with Reid. He was deep in discussion with the fire chief; she hung back, waiting until it was obvious that their conversation was ending before she moved forward.

'...especially in the north-east corner, around what's left of the organ,' she heard the fire chief say to Reid. 'We think that's what started the fire, and it burned longest and hardest in that area. You'll see the most damage there and up overhead, where there's one Sunday school classroom that's probably not safe. Here, you'll need this,' he finished, handing an impressively large flashlight to Reid, then moved aside the saw-horse barrier by the steps, permitting them to enter.

Inside, beyond the reach of the sun, they were surrounded by a damp dark cold and the acrid odour of charred wood. Clearly the fire hadn't reached this point: the narthex was undamaged, although the walls and ceiling bore a heavy covering of grimy smoke and there were puddles of dirty water—now frozen—on the floor.

'Grim,' Reid observed with brief economy, the word echoing hollowly in the darkness. He moved forward, Kathy lagging behind, to open the double doors at the end of the centre aisle. 'Even worse here. You think this is worth saving?'

'Yes,' she answered steadily, in spite of the sight which greeted her.

There was more light in this large space, but only because of the sunlight flooding in where the far left corner of the building had been destroyed. The slip pews—part of some earlier attempt to modernise, Kathy noted—were still mostly in their neat rows; otherwise, the devastation appeared complete. Much of the ceiling had fallen, and roof beams and rafters had come crashing down; their charred lengths lay at crazy angles, stark fingers of destruction pointing to the sky. In the sanctuary, above what remained of the altar, the jagged remnants of a stained glass window caught the sun, reflecting a crazy quilt of colours on the ruined floor, near where one particularly large beam had scored a direct hit on the pulpit.

'It's enough to make you believe in divine retribution,' Reid remarked, grim humour in his voice. 'If I were Father Gardiner, I'd be afraid to preach another sermon.'

'But baptisms seem safe enough,' Kathy contributed with humour of her own, pointing to the font which still stood, untouched and serene, amid the wreckage.

'No, not yet,' he told her when she would have advanced into the centre aisle, his hand closing on her wrist to draw her back. 'Before we move around in here, we'll check what's up above.'

'It looks safe enough.'

'That's a matter of opinion.' When she tried to pull free, his grip tightened, holding her firmly in place. 'Overhead, you've got the steeple to consider——'

'The fire didn't reach the steeple.'

'Are you sure of that? I doubt that there are any fire stops, which means that the fire could have run through the walls to weaken the steeple supports,' he pointed out, crisp and professional. 'There's a lot of weight up there—the bell and the old clock. You may be willing to take a chance that the whole thing won't come crashing down, but I'd rather not.'

'All right.' She nodded, waiting for him to release her wrist, wondering why he didn't. 'Sorry,' she finally added.

'So you should be . . . although why I should care what happens to you is a mystery to me.' He permitted himself a brief smile, one which surprised her by reaching his eyes, before—without warning—he banished the smile and relaxed his grip. 'How can we get up to the steeple?' he asked, the cool professional once again.

'There should be stairs here,' she answered, rubbing at her wrist, trying to erase the lingering memory of the imprint of his fingers. Grateful for an excuse to move away from him, she began to examine the panelling on the north side of the narthex. 'Here, I think,' she called out when she'd found the latch hidden under its thick coating of soot. She pulled open the door, waiting until Reid directed the flashlight's beam into the darkness. 'Yes,' she breathed when she saw the narrow, twisting flight of stairs. 'These are the original.'

'How can you tell?'

She shrugged. 'They just look right—steep enough, the newel post very simple... It's like pie crust,' she tried to explain. 'The recipe can't tell you when it's ready to be rolled out. You just have to know.'

'Spare me,' he said, his expression pained. 'Are your conclusions always this vague?'

'No,' she flared, defensive. 'I can often be very precise, but restoration work isn't engineering. A lot of it has to be guesswork—and judgement based on experience.'

'Of which you've had so much,' he jeered.

'In certain areas, I've had quite a bit!'

'And old churches are your speciality,' he continued, a decided edge to his voice. 'Incredibly convenient, isn't it? A heaven-sent opportunity—pardon the pun—to get close to my aunt.'

'I didn't need an opportunity!' Kathy snapped. 'We were already close!'

'That's hard to believe—given that she's never mentioned you——'

'Because I asked her not to!'

'Why? Because you didn't want me to know what game you were playing?'

'I didn't want you to know anything about me, and I didn't want to know anything about you,' Kathy retaliated fiercely. 'Aunt Margaret understood that—and there was no game!'

'No?' Negligently, he leaned against the wall—today's pristine chinos were going to be filthy, Kathy thought, perversely pleased. 'She doesn't have any real money, you know. She's been spending capital for years; there's almost none left.'

'Why should I...?' Kathy stopped dead, drew a long, sharp breath. 'You can't seriously think I'm after her money?'

'You always did like your creature comforts.'

'That's a damned lie, and you know it!'

'Swearing in church, Kath?' He shook his head, making a game of mocking her. 'What would the good people of East Hawley think of that?'

'I don't give a damn what they—or you!—think, and if you got me in here just so you could have fun insulting me... Well, I won't have it!' In the gloom, she started to move past him, making for the stairs.

'I've got the flashlight,' he reminded her. 'Better let me go first.'

'Then go!'

Seething silently, she followed behind him, nearly running into his large frame when he stopped, without warning, on the top step.

'It's some kind of a balcony——'

'A gallery,' she corrected sharply, pleased for the opportunity to score even a small point. 'Originally, there would have been galleries running down both sides, plus one in the middle. It's not unusual to find the side galleries closed in—for storage or classrooms—and the rear one left open for a choir loft.'

'It looks as if that's what we've got here,' he told her, turning back to her; then, burying the hatchet, at least for the moment, he added, 'It seems you really do know your stuff.'

'I try,' she answered briefly, breaking eye contact to look past him, into the gallery. 'Would you move?'

'Right.' Obligingly, he took the final step, slowly playing the flashlight's beam around the open space. 'No sign of fire here,' he reported when he was done, moving aside to permit her to join him. 'Is there any way to get into the steeple?'

'On the outside wall there should be a ladder and a trapdoor. If you're going up, you're on your own. I don't like ladders or heights.'

'Don't tell me!' In the moment before he turned towards the ladder, she caught his mocking smile. 'You're willing to admit that something frightens you?'

'Makes me uncomfortable,' she corrected carefully. 'Nothing really frightens me.'

What a lie! she thought as he started up the ladder and disappeared into the gloom. She went to the railing, staring blindly down into the ruined nave. Once she could have said it and believed it; after what Reid had done to her, after all she'd been through, she had been beyond fear... or so she'd thought. Now, she knew better. After less than an hour here inside the church, she was frightened of Reid.

There was something so contradictory about him. He was still as attractive—no denying that!—although in a more seasoned and mature way. Eight years, after all, had worked nearly as much of a change in him as it had in her, but it wasn't his physical appeal which frightened her. It was the way he was treating her, the lightning changes in his mood. His hostility was hard to take, particularly when there was absolutely no reason why he should bear her any animosity!

After all, she'd left without a fuss, hadn't she? She'd asked for nothing, made no demands... just quietly removed herself from his life. She was the injured party in this mess; he had no reason to be angry—unless her unexpected presence seemed to him a reproach.

As well it should! she assured herself with rising indignation. After the way he'd treated her, he had every reason to feel guilty, and if the only way he had to handle it was by being a perfect beast... Well, that was his problem, not hers! No, it wasn't his anger she found most difficult to handle. It was the rare glimpse of something else, something less tangible... like their exchange just now, on the stairs—when he'd suddenly treated her with respect. She hadn't trusted either one of them in that moment; it wasn't the way things had ever been between the two of them, the way things should be now...

'There's no sign of fire up there, no sign that any of the load-bearing members have weakened.'

At the sound of his voice, Kathy had to control a faint flutter of nerves, had to force herself to face him again. 'So we're in no danger of being crushed?'

'I'd say so. Next, we'd better check those two—what did you call them?—galleries. This one shouldn't have suffered any damage.' He moved away, used his light to find the door. 'It looks as if there's stuff stored in here.'

'Really?' Kathy felt a quick flare of excitement. 'Let me see!'

Obligingly, he aimed the light, revealing the crazy jumble which filled the long narrow space. 'Plenty of dust and plenty of soot,' he noted as Kathy slipped past him to inspect what was nearest.

'Pews,' she breathed, running her hands over one surface, then another. 'Look! Shine the light here... do you see?' She rubbed her sleeve across a small raised oval, removing most of the grime. 'Yes! It's the number——'

'Thirty-two,' Reid deciphered for her. 'Is that important?'

'What's important is that these must be the remains of the original pews. They were numbered, back then. People had to pay for their pews; they were personal property. This is fantastic!' She moved deeper into the storage space, snaking her way through the untidy stacks. 'This almost never happens, but I've got to believe they're all here, and—oh! Reid, see this—the Palladian window, probably the one from over the altar, where the stained glass one is now.'

'What remains of it,' Reid corrected. 'Which isn't much.'

'Thank goodness! Stained glass doesn't belong in this type of church,' she explained when she saw Reid's questioning look, 'and, since this one's been destroyed, we can use the Palladian in the restoration.'

'*If* there's a restoration,' Reid cautioned. 'Some people want to tear everything down and start over.'

'Yes, but I'm hoping I can change their minds,' she confessed. 'It would be a shame to lose this fine an example, unless the parish can't afford to do anything but tear it down and put up something cheap. If that's the case, it wouldn't be fair of me to urge them to keep this.'

'Fair?' Reid questioned, his tone mocking her. 'Don't tell me you've acquired some principles?'

'Acquired?' she managed before her voice choked on a fierce surge of anger. She turned away, out of the glare of his flashlight, drew a deep and steadying breath. 'If you understood me as well as you think you do, you'd know that I've always had principles. Nothing has changed!'

'Of course not,' he agreed smoothly, but she knew he wasn't convinced. The tension between them was again just as high—nothing had changed about that!

Now they worked almost without speaking—only the bare minimum to get the job done. Reid checked for fire damage and assessed structural integrity, while she took careful notes of original details and design features. Finally, in the gallery on the opposite side, they paused by the closed door of the last of the three small classrooms which shared the enclosed space.

'We know there's fire damage beyond this point,' Reid noted, his hand on the doorknob, 'but we'd better see just how bad it is.'

He opened the door and sunlight poured in, an assault of brilliance after the gloom of the enclosed gallery.

Briefly, they were both blinded, then Reid stepped gingerly over the threshold, Kathy right behind him.

'Not much left,' he commented.

'But look at what is left,' she insisted and they stood side by side to survey this most damaged end of the building. Almost all of the two outside walls had disappeared, as well as most of the roof. All that remained was an irregular section of floor, the rugged corner post and a few of the beams and rafters above, minus their roof-boards and shingles.

'Nothing to save in this corner,' Reid decided with a dismissive gesture.

'But I can see how the roof was constructed. Look at those beautiful rafters,' she marvelled, moving a cautious foot or two forward. 'It's a wonder that the fire didn't bring them all down!' The large spans—nearly a foot thick—had endured, thanks to the careful bevelling of each edge. Badly charred, they were silhouetted against the blue sky, stark lines and angles... 'There's something different about them,' she breathed, moving still further forward, craning her neck to see more. 'They're pitched! They——'

She heard a sharp noise—a kind of cracking sound—and felt an instant's disorientation, as though the world had begun to shift on its axis. 'Kath, don't—for heaven's sake!' That was Reid's voice, harsh and impatient; she started to turn, to see what was the matter, and suddenly her right arm was being pulled—nearly out of the socket, she decided when the pain hit her.

'For heaven's sake,' Reid said again, just as she collided with him, the impact with his hard form knocking all the breath from her. He swore fluently, and she lost her footing as he wrapped both arms around her and drew her back through the doorway, into the gloom. 'Fool! Why didn't you think?' he demanded.

'Think——' she got out, desperate for air, her left hand pushing ineffectually against his chest '—what?'

'You damn near fell through,' he explained, sounding nearly as short of breath as she did. 'If I hadn't been able to grab your arm...'

So that's what had happened—nearly happened, she amended, capable of more coherent thought when he relaxed his hold on her just enough to permit her to draw a deep breath. Now at least some of her random impressions made sense, although she didn't understand why he was still holding her close—or why she was letting him do it. And why was her hand still on his chest, feeling the racing beat of his heart?

'Reid,' she whispered, staring up at him, her eyes wide with alarm. 'We——'

'Don't,' he murmured, his voice deeper than usual, a little rougher. 'Don't say it.'

'Don't say what?' she managed, but it was hard—hard to concentrate on anything but his heartbeat and the fact that her body was moulded against the unyielding strength of his, the heat of him searing her. This was madness! she tried to tell herself, a madness they shared...and always had, she remembered—remembering, too, the clean, masculine scent of him, and the way his lower lip always curved when he was about to kiss her. 'Reid,' she attempted half-heartedly, 'we shouldn't...'

'I know,' he acknowledged, but he didn't release her, and she knew she was lost.

They both were, she realised as his hands smoothed down her back to draw her more gently to him. He bent his head; his lips briefly touched hers, then returned, wanting more—what she wanted, too, she acknowledged dreamily. This was what she wanted, what she needed...his kiss and his touch.

'Yes,' she whispered as she reached up to link her arms around his neck, then her breath caught on a swift dart of pain.

'Your arm?' he asked quickly, his self-possession instantly intact again—as was hers, she discovered, and felt a momentary twinge of regret. 'Is it painful?'

'Yes, just a little,' she told him, drawing back as soon as he released her, letting her left arm cradle her right.

'Sorry about that,' he offered—a dual apology—with a cool twist of a smile.

'It's all right.' She paused, then added with meaning, proving she was equally cool, 'Just as well that it hurt when it did.'

'Still,' he began, clear warning in his voice, 'we can't avoid the fact that at least one thing hasn't changed between us.'

No, some things hadn't changed, Kathy brooded a few moments later, standing alone in the sunshine while Reid conferred with the fire chief. The current between them—that madness of attraction—had always been there. At the start, she hadn't immediately recognised it for what it was. That time, she'd been naïve enough to believe that attraction was love; now she knew better. Inside the church, when Reid had pulled her to safety, her body had briefly betrayed her—her body, but nothing else!

What had happened meant nothing, changed nothing of how she felt about Reid! she assured herself, fiercely determined. What had happened was just... an unfortunate lapse, she decided, an accident. They had simply got too close; from now on, she'd make sure she didn't wander into that kind of danger. She'd keep her distance, and she was pretty sure that Reid would keep his...

'Coming?' he asked with cool brevity, not waiting for her response before striding off across the green, heading back to Aunt Margaret's house.

He was no happier about what had happened than she was, she concluded, making no effort to catch up with him. She'd caught only a glimpse of his face, but his expression had been grim enough—features rigidly without expression, even a slight hint of grey beneath his deep tan. Obviously, it had been a real shock to his system, she mused on a hard edge of bitter humour. He didn't like the idea that he was still attracted to the girl he'd rejected so many years before... Well, isn't that just too bad! she thought with a defiant toss of her head. If he thinks I like it any better than he does, he's dead wrong!

She took her time crossing the green after him, perversely pleased to see him waiting impatiently for her on the far side of the road. 'I don't know why you didn't go in without me,' she told him when she finally caught up.

He shot her a quick black glance. 'I wanted to be sure you remember to keep your personal feelings under control——'

'*My* personal feelings?' she broke in indignantly, rewarded with a second black look.

'All right, then—we'll keep *our* personal feelings under control—is that better?'

'More accurate, anyway,' she observed tartly, and saw his lips tighten. Good! she told herself, pleased that he didn't like being reminded of that little scene—any more than she did. 'We'll both be happier if we keep our personal feelings under control.'

'At the moment, I'm only thinking of my aunt,' he bit out, still angry. 'To know just how things are between us would distress her.'

But it was Emma who greeted them at the door; Aunt Margaret was nowhere to be seen. 'She's at church,' Emma explained in response to Reid's question. 'The Methodists took them in.'

'I didn't know...' Kathy bit her lip, worried it briefly. 'Perhaps I should have gone, too.'

'I don't see why,' Emma objected flatly. 'Your soul's in no danger today—they'll do enough praying for you, and Mr Reid, too. After all, you're their one hope at the moment.'

'There's reality for you,' Reid observed appreciatively—so he could be pleasant, if only to other people,

Kathy noted with asperity. 'You sound like a true disbeliever.'

'No. Just a solitary believer,' Emma amplified with precision. 'God and I manage better when we're left alone. Do you two want some coffee?' she asked, ending the theological discussion in an abrupt switch. 'And there's been a telephone call for you, Miss Kathy. You're to call Luce, just as soon as you can.'

'Luce?' Reid repeated, looking at Kathy with a questioning gaze. 'An admirer?'

'A young lady,' Emma corrected. 'One with a strange accent.'

'She's a Texan,' Kathy explained absently, looking around for the phone.

'In the front hall,' Emma directed, providing Kathy with a way to remove herself from Reid's presence.

'Malcolm called,' Luce began as soon as she heard Kathy's voice. 'Last night, in fact—just before ten, which shows what he thinks you have going for you as a social life... Not that he hasn't already made that pretty clear. I told him I didn't know where you were.'

'Why did you do that?' Kathy wailed.

'To put him in his place,' Luce explained briskly. 'It's about time he realised that there's more to you than your job.'

'Which there isn't, not really,' Kathy put in quickly—honestly, too. For the first time in years, though, the idea bothered her just a bit: it sounded so dull! 'What did he want?'

'You, naturally,' Luce responded, her pronounced drawl heavy with sarcasm, 'to check a few things for him. I told him that I didn't think you'd be able to be much help, but that I'd pass on the message—*if* you got in touch with me.'

'He left his number?' Kathy asked quickly. He'd given it to her before he'd left Providence; in her haste to get to Aunt Margaret, it had been left behind, somewhere among the blizzard of papers on the desk in her bedroom. 'If——'

'He left it,' Luce interrupted, 'but I gave you the perfect excuse. You don't have to call!'

'Well, I'm going to,' Kathy all but snapped, angry not with Luce but with herself. To have forgotten all about Malcolm was out of character, something that had never happened before...

CHAPTER FOUR

IT WAS all Reid's fault, Kathy concluded, dialling Malcolm's number. Seeing Reid, being forced to confront him, had knocked everything else out of her head. She wasn't reacting normally at the moment, but a little time talking to Malcolm would take care of that! Malcolm was as unlike Reid as could be imagined; Malcolm was steady, deliberate, precise, a man who avoided extremes. Malcolm rarely laughed, but to balance that lack he never really got angry. Of course, Kathy conceded, there were times when he was unable to prevent his irritation from showing . . . and this was one of those times, she knew as soon as she heard him answer the phone.

'Malcolm, I'm terribly sorry,' she plunged in immediately. 'Luce should have——'

'Where are you?'

'In Vermont. East Hawley—not that the name will mean anything to you. It's a very small town . . .' She was babbling, she realised with a grimace, knowing how much Malcolm disliked idle chatter. 'The thing is, Malcolm, their church burned yesterday—no, day before, I think. You may have seen it in the papers,' she hurried on, unconsciously drawing on part of Aunt Margaret's presentation. 'It made the front page——'

'Of the *New York Times*?' Malcolm cut in smoothly. 'I doubt it.'

'I suppose you're right about that,' she allowed, then grasped at a straw—after all, didn't making the front page somewhere confer some importance on the event? 'It did make the front page in Providence——'

'And the firm has already been contacted?' Malcolm asked, overriding her words. 'The parishioners want a consultation?'

'Well, not exactly,' Kathy admitted uncomfortably. 'It's quite informal, at this point. You see, one of the members is an old friend of mine——'

'Friendship, Kathy?' Malcolm enquired, his arch smile audible in his tone. 'How many times have I told you that friendship and business simply don't mix? I've turned down fine commissions, when the request came from a friend, and while this is a bit different—I presume your friend is no one I know?'

'Oh, no. Not at——'

'Then even though this is a bit different,' Malcolm prevailed, 'I'm afraid that the firm will simply have to refuse the business.'

'But that's just it, Malcolm.' She hesitated, to gather her thoughts—something she ought to have done in the first place; she should have appealed to Malcolm's academic interest. 'This may be a significant church. I think——'

'Kathy, it doesn't matter what you think,' Malcolm interrupted in his most repressive tone, 'and it doesn't matter how significant the church may be. The firm does not mix business with friendship. We are not taking it on.'

'But that's just it,' she told him. 'It's not business, and the firm isn't taking it on. I am.'

'It's the same thing.'

'No, not this time, Malcolm,' she insisted. 'I'm just doing this, a little bit of preliminary work, as a favour to—to my friend.'

'And what, exactly, does that mean?'

'Just that I've gone through the church, seen what's there, and drawn some conclusions. Tonight——'

'Kathy,' he broke in impatiently, 'how long are you going to be stuck there?'

'Just a couple of days,' Kathy assured him. 'I might even be leaving tomorrow——'

'Well, that's a relief! I was afraid you intended to stay indefinitely, and I wasn't at all sure how I would manage. Kathy, you really are indispensable to me . . . I'm not at all sure how I'd get along without you, my dear.'

'Oh.' It was enough of a declaration to render her speechless; no matter how much Malcolm depended on her, he rarely admitted it to her. Even less frequently did he call her 'my dear'. That expression was reserved for the times which passed for intimate moments between them; it was not a term Malcolm used lightly, and he'd never used it before on the phone! 'Thank you, Malcolm,' she finally managed. 'That's very sweet——'

'It's true,' he said firmly. 'Surely you know how I feel by this time?'

'Well, yes, I suppose . . . It's just——'

'So, don't let yourself become too deeply involved with this church—or this friend,' he added with meaning. 'If you're not back tomorrow, I might begin to be just a little jealous of this friend of yours.'

'What? Oh, Malcolm!' Kathy smothered a giggle, thinking that this was more like it; the gentle, almost courtly teasing was what she expected of Malcolm—a game the two of them enjoyed playing. 'You don't need to worry,' she promised him, laughter lingering to colour her words. 'My friend's a very dear and very elderly lady—no reason for you to be jealous!'

'Good. I'm pleased to hear that. Now look . . .' He paused, then continued more briskly, 'I'm going to be at least two more weeks here—it's an immensely more complicated project than we could have imagined—but I may take a quick run back to Providence on Tuesday or Wednesday . . . just to make sure that you kept your word.'

'But I will,' she volunteered quickly. 'You don't need to worry.'

'Still, I could use a few hours with you, in the office, then we might go out for an early dinner. What do you say?'

'It sounds lovely. I'll be looking forward to it.'

'The meal? Or seeing me?'

'Seeing you, of course,' she answered promptly.

'Fine! Until then,' he promised. 'Until Tuesday or Wednesday, my dear.'

Two 'my dears' in the same conversation! she marvelled, her cup overflowing. It was far more than she had any right to expect, unless... Perhaps he really had felt he had reason to worry; after all, this was the first time in six years that she'd gone off on her own—without even trying to get in touch with him to tell him her plans. Such a totally unexpected—and unprecedented!—burst of independence must have surprised him... In which case, she might try it again, she decided with a quick smile. 'Yes, until then, Malcolm,' she told him, still smiling, 'and thank you!'

'Think nothing of it, my dear,' he responded kindly, then ended the call.

'My dear,' Kathy thought, foolishly cradling the now dead receiver. 'My dear'—not once, not twice, but three times in the same conversation... Incredible!

'Malcolm?' Reid enquired from behind her, his voice coolly amused. '"Until then"—to someone named Malcolm?'

'You were listening,' she accused, as she turned to find him, coffee-mug in one hand, leaning with negligent ease against the doorjamb. 'You had no right!'

He shrugged. 'It wasn't intentional. I was on my way up to my room, and I hated to just barge on through.'

'So you just stood there and listened!'

'It was hard not to.' He smiled—nothing friendly or pleasant about it; his smile mocked her, dismissed her feelings as unimportant. 'I gather that Malcolm supplies the romance in your life.'

'He's my boss,' Kathy snapped, then wishing she'd said nothing.

'I see.' Reid paused to sip his coffee. 'Is that why he almost never lets you finish a sentence?'

'He does,' she insisted, but her eyes slid away from the idea of meeting Reid's gaze.

'He didn't today. What is it? Are you supposed to play submissive female in his male dominance game?'

'It's not like that,' Kathy muttered, eyes flashing. 'You don't understand.'

'I'd say it was Malcolm who didn't,' Reid observed sagely, then took another sip of his coffee, speculatively regarding her over the rim of his mug. 'Still, I suppose it might suit you to let Malcolm think he's got you under his thumb. He's your boss, so he's the main chance. Fancy yourself the half-owner of a restoration business, do you?'

'I don't have to answer that!'

'You don't need to. The answer's obvious,' he told her, angry for the first time, his words clipped and cold. 'You're amazing, Kath! Unstoppable, I'd say—at least until now—but don't you ever suffer at least a twinge of conscience?'

'I don't need to,' she answered steadily, no problem now in meeting his eyes. Whatever he'd done to try to rationalise his own behaviour, *she* was the innocent in all of this! 'I don't know what you're thinking——'

'About unfinished business, all those messy details you've been avoiding for years.'

'The same ones *you've* been avoiding?' she was stung to demand. 'What's the difference?'

'Offhand, I'd say Malcolm, for one,' Reid responded, a dangerous spark in his eyes. 'Do you really think you're being fair to dear Malcolm?'

'Whether I am or not is no business of yours!'

'You think not?' He left the support of the doorjamb to move closer to her—stalking her, like a sleek but powerful jungle cat, she thought uneasily, afraid to move when he leaned forward, invading her space to place his coffee-mug on the telephone stand. 'Some people might disagree,' he continued, still too close for comfort, speaking softly, but with a hard, bitter edge to his words. 'Some people might say it was nobody's business *but* mine... What would Malcolm say, do you think?'

'I——' she began, but her throat was so dry that she was forced to swallow and start again. 'I don't care,' she finally managed, knowing instantly—even before she saw his sardonic smile, or the unholy glitter in his silver gaze—that she'd said the wrong thing.

'I know you don't care, Kath. You never have... but Malcolm might, don't you think? What would he think of that moment, back at the church?'

'That was nothing!'

'Nothing?' he asked with cool irony. 'You sell yourself short, Kath. My response was considerably more than nothing...and your response felt like more than nothing to me.'

'But it *meant* nothing,' she insisted, fighting a rising panic. He was moving closer—too close!—crowding her back against the edge of the telephone stand, holding her captive. 'It was just—just chemistry.'

'That's right,' he agreed, his face only inches from hers now, his breath stirring her hair, 'and it's powerful stuff, isn't it? Hard to fight...'

'Reid, don't,' she protested weakly, but it was already too late—for either of them, she supposed as his lips captured hers. What drove them made no sense; they hated each other, yet craved this kind of intimacy... Chemistry! she despaired, her resolution swept away by the fierce demand of his kiss, by her own mindless need to respond. It was all so familiar, so like the past... She was melting, her body on fire, yet possessed by a delicious languor, alive now, in a way she hadn't been for so many years... It didn't matter, she tried telling herself, that this was wrong—but it *did* matter! It was what she had wanted—at all cost—to avoid, too dangerous...

'Damn you,' she said, wrenching herself away from the tyranny of temptation, slipping sideways, retreating to the foot of the stairs to put a safe distance between them. 'I will never forgive you for this!'

'Forgive me?' he enquired, his self-possession instantly in place again, his voice carrying nothing more than a hint of jaded amusement. 'Or yourself? Don't forget—it takes two, and you were willing, more than willing, I'd say.' He smiled, mocking her. 'What's between us is always going to be there... Always, Kathy...'

She'd heard enough, and the stairs were there for her retreat... but she wouldn't—couldn't—forget.

It had always been there between them—chemistry!—although Kathy hadn't known it until they were finally alone on his boat. Even then, she had tried to find some other excuse for what had happened. Proximity had seemed a good choice; the boat was, after all, very small. There was a minimal galley, with room for only one person, the head, the cramped salon and one nearly claustrophobic cabin, which Reid had given to her, as he was already using the berth in the salon.

And that was it—the smallest boat she'd ever been on, Kathy mused, going down to the cabin when they'd left the island behind and there was nothing left to see—not even a dark speck on the horizon. How long, she wondered, would it be until they reached an island where he could leave her? Curaçao and Aruba were the closest, but perhaps he didn't intend to head for either of them.

In fact, she had no idea what course he was setting; she hadn't bothered to ask him, hadn't cared. It was enough to know that she'd found a way off the island; sorting out the rest of it—with the frightening demands of independence and the need to be self-supporting—could wait for another day. Well, yes—another day, she thought, but never another week. It wouldn't be that long. She only had a few days to plan her future—something she was only now beginning to realise she should have thought through thoroughly before she'd made this wild move!

A few days... so no need to really unpack her things, she decided, rummaging through her one bulging duffel bag for the necessities she'd need for these few days. A few pairs of shorts, a few T-shirts, the small bag of toiletries and her toothbrush, her nightgown... Briefly, her hands were still; she shivered, remembering the previous night, the way she had felt when Reid had fastened the gold necklace for her, the way it had felt to stand so close to him...

Anything else? she asked herself briskly, her thoughts tripping over themselves in her haste to get away from that memory. Yes, underwear; then her hands paused once again, to rest on her bright green bikini. Should she? she wondered doubtfully, then told herself not to be silly. She was sure to want it some time; she was tempted to wear it now. Already, even this early in the morning, it was hot enough; besides, bikinis were practically a norm, she assured herself—no one gave them a thought!

Reid did, though; she knew it as soon as she appeared on deck. In spite of his dark glasses, she could feel his gaze—concentrated and intense—on her, although his words were casual. 'If that's all you're going to wear, you'd better put on sun screen.'

'I don't need it. I'm lucky, I never burn,' she explained, coming to stand beside him in the cockpit, casually checking the instruments. 'This is as dark as I get,' she added, almost apologetically, glancing down, comparing her light honey-gold to his deep brown.

He was wearing shorts, faded denim cut-offs which offered her the opportunity to study the impressive length of his legs—teak-brown, with a scattering of fine dark hairs, hard-corded muscles, their latent power obvious... even dangerous, she realised. She turned away, pretending to scan the horizon while she fought the sudden dryness in her throat, then asked abruptly, 'Do you want some coffee?'

'Why not?' The words were barely audible, but she could hear the lazy amusement in his voice—as though he knew what she was thinking.

She fled to the galley, took longer than she needed to make two mugs of instant. Don't be silly! she scolded herself, waiting for the pot to boil. There's nothing between us—there won't be anything between us! He's just a friend—no, not even really a friend. He's just someone willing to take you off the island; he's an older man, for heaven's sake! Just because he's incredibly attractive—the only man you've ever noticed in quite that way—it doesn't mean that anything will happen. You're a child to him; he's not interested in you for—for things like that!

But all that day she watched him. Greedily, she absorbed every detail, noted, beneath the tautly stretched, deep blue T-shirt, the breadth of his shoulders, the way the muscles bunched and rippled as he moved; she studied the paradoxical spare economy and sensuous grace of his movements, the way his hands closed around a coffee-mug, the quick transformation of his features when he smiled...

He took a long first watch in the night, calling down to rouse her for hers. 'Coffee?' he suggested—his turn to offer—when she joined him in the darkness.

She nodded, her breath catching when they changed places and his lean, hard form brushed against her softer curves. Briefly alone, she studied the stars—brilliant, cool pinpoints of light against the blackness all around. Alone, she thought; we're all alone in time and space...and anything could happen now.

'Here.' He was back, a long dark shadow in the greater darkness, his fingers touching hers when he passed the mug to her. 'A fine night,' he observed, nothing of what she was feeling in his tone.

'Yes...wonderful,' she managed, her words a breathless whisper in the dark.

'Did you sleep?'

'Yes.' A lie! She bent her head to sip from the mug. It had been too hot, too close, in the tiny cabin. She had stretched out on the berth, lying rigid in the darkness, listening for the slightest sound of him, wanting to go up and join him, wanting—needing!—to be with him.

'Nearly dawn,' he'd noted, his voice dry, without expression. He drained his mug, then stretched, smothering a yawn. 'My turn to sleep. My alarm's built in, so you won't need to wake me.'

To wake him! she thought, her pulse stumbling then picking up a faster beat. To come upon him unawares, to lean towards him in the darkness, to reach out her hand and touch his arm or his shoulder, to lay her palm against his cheek... He'd become a fever in her blood, a consuming passion. She wanted more of him than he would ever guess, more then she could ever have, she reminded herself sharply.

That day, her wakeful night caught up with her. Between her watches, she slept on the deck—sleek and catlike, soaking up the sun.

'Get up, lazybones,' he teased, coming to rouse her in the late afternoon, 'or you'll never sleep tonight.'

'I don't care.' She turned, stretching luxuriously, smiling up at him, pleased that he had, for the first time today, abandoned the dark glasses which had hidden his eyes from her. 'I can take your night watch, if you like.'

'Why not?' he agreed carelessly, but there was nothing careless in the way he was looking at her. His silver gaze had darkened, had shaded into grey; it was sharper, more intense, beneath heavy lids. 'I could do with a good night's sleep.'

'Then it's settled.' She sat up, suddenly closer to him than she had been, only inches away, in fact. 'It's got hotter, hasn't it?' she asked, turning away from him to face the empty horizon. 'Almost too hot.' She lifted her hair, knowing he was watching every move she made. Now the power was with her, she realised, smiling to herself. 'Could we swim? Just for a few minutes?' she coaxed, turning quickly back to him.

'Of course,' he agreed easily enough, but she caught the edge of hunger in his eyes before he reached for his dark glasses and slipped them on. 'You can, but I'll watch.'

'You won't come with me?' she appealed, her hand briefly touching his. 'I thought——'

He shook his head. 'I never leave the boat unmanned, and no one swims without someone looking out.'

'Then we'll never swim together.'

'We'll survive,' he told her, laughter in his voice—his poise intact again, she realised—offering his hand to draw her to her feet. 'I'll go after you.'

'All right.' Depression settled over her. This wasn't what she wanted, what she'd planned. She'd had some half-formed fantasy: the two of them together in the water, somehow coming together, somehow... Well, she wasn't really sure about the details, but somehow...

She stopped that thought by diving cleanly, the water cold against her heated skin, the shock enough to drive dangerous imaginings from her mind.

She was a good swimmer. Her father had been fond of saying that she'd learned to swim before she'd learned to walk—a slight exaggeration, but not by much. Now she struck out, knifing through the water; in physical activity, she found release from her wayward and reckless thoughts. Several times she swam around the boat, each time the circle growing wider, and she watched Reid's slow turns as he kept her in sight.

'You're good,' he called out to her when she finally paused to tread water and catch her breath, 'but don't you think you've had enough?'

She shook her head. 'I'm a fish,' she called back, then drew one last deep breath and executed a shallow dive, beginning an even wider circle. She could stay here all day, she thought, exulting in the sensuous slip, the cool caress, of the water; she could stay here all day...until the sunset stained the water glittering shades of crimson and gold...until twilight brought deepening shades of violet and indigo...until nightfall changed the water to black satin and the reflected starlight attached itself to the surface...

'That was grand,' she gasped, thoroughly out of breath when she finally turned back to the boat. She had worked the edginess out of her system. The strange discontent and vague longing were gone now. They were pointless feelings, even silly and childish; Reid was, after all, just a friend, she reminded herself, treading water while he fixed the ladder over the side for her. 'Thanks.' She smiled up at him as she climbed the ladder, accepting his hand to help her on to the deck. She'd left the buoyancy of the water behind her; now she stumbled as the deck's gentle rocking movement caught her off balance.

Instantly, his hands were on her arms to steady her. 'All right?'

'Yes, but I think...' She stopped, and there was a long, timeless silence between them. His hands were still on her arms—his warmth against her cool, salty skin—and her pulse was already racing out of control. It was too late, she knew, even before she saw the fire in his silver-grey eyes; too late to turn back, too late to stop what had been between them from the start...

'Kathy—I can't help this,' he confessed, his voice a rough murmur as he drew her close—the length of his body meeting hers, the two of them joined.

The contact, the contrast, was a shock—his fire against her ice, she told herself; his fire warming her, and his kiss... Openly, eagerly, she met his kiss and returned it—and felt her defences beginning to crumble. I must stop him—or myself—she thought, before things go too far... But it was hard—much too hard!—and hadn't she already known that it was too late? He was already too important, too vital to her existence, and surely that meant that this was love!

That makes it all right! she decided fiercely, casting restraint to the winds, losing herself in the magic his hands and his lips were creating, learning ways to please him from the ways he was pleasing her. Of course this is love! she promised herself in her last conscious thought before Reid and this new world he was creating—all sensation, desire and need—took complete possession of her.

Later—much later—she had fallen asleep in his gentle embrace, had awakened to find the sky painted violet and deep indigo. Just as she'd imagined it, a few hours ago—no, a lifetime ago, she corrected with a slow smile. What had happened, what Reid had shared with her, was the start of a new lifetime. Now the first eighteen empty, meaningless years were in the past; Reid had made a new person of her—a woman, she decided after a moment's reflection. She had started this day as a girl, was ending it as a woman.

'Kathy...' Reid spoke in the gathering darkness; had she given him some slight sign that she was awake? she wondered, or was it simply that they were so close now—so bound together—that he *knew*? 'You might have told me.'

'Told you what?' she asked lazily.

'You know very well what.' She felt him stir, opened her eyes to find him leaning over her, searching her face. 'That you were such a complete innocent.'

She bit her lip. His words sounded, she thought, like a reproach or an accusation. 'I didn't think,' she offered inadequately. 'I'm sorry.'

'Sorry for what?'

'That...' He wasn't going to make it any easier for her, she noted, all her happiness instantly gone, replaced by bitter shame. 'That I haven't had any experience,' she forced herself to explain. 'That I didn't know what to do.'

'You're dead wrong,' he countered, his soft laughter taking her by surprise. 'My dear, you're a natural at this sort of thing... beyond my wildest expectations.'

'Really?' she asked in breathless wonder. This was not what she'd expected; it was hard to believe... 'Am I really?'

'Yes, you really are,' he assured her, his tone teasing, indulgent. 'Believe it, Kathy—you're a natural,' he said again, 'delightfully uninhibited... marvellously inventive——'

'A quick learner,' she suggested, his praise making her bold, 'and taught by a master.'

'You think so? I'm not so sure,' he told her, his expression detached, giving nothing away. 'What you have is special, but it was just waiting——'

'For you,' she put in quickly. 'Don't think—I couldn't have been like this with—with...'

'With any man,' he finally supplied for her, ignoring—or unaware of—her acute embarrassment. 'No, not with just any man, but you're still new at the game, sweet Kath, so don't make the mistake of thinking I'm the only one who can make you feel this way.'

'But you are! Because of who you are,' she said fiercely. This was wrong! she thought. She couldn't, she *wouldn't* let him convince her—or himself—that this was anything but special! 'You've got to understand,' she insisted, reaching out to him. 'I couldn't have let someone else... It's because of *you*!'

'Perhaps,' he allowed, not so detached this time, 'and this much is true...' He bent his head; his lips briefly touched hers. 'There's powerful stuff between us... and hard to fight,' he added, his lips returning for an endless moment, savouring her quick response. 'And it's always going to be there,' he promised as he drew her closer and his hands began to move on her skin. 'Always, Kathy. Always...'

The same words! Kathy realised, her nerves stretched nearly to the breaking-point; all these years later, he was still using the same words as though he'd forgotten nothing of that first time. Just as she'd forgotten nothing, she admitted reluctantly. She'd pushed it away, blocked it off in a far corner of her mind, refused to remember for almost eight years, but it had always been there—just waiting to trip her up, she brooded.

She didn't like remembering that kind of thing. She hated admitting the power he'd had over her—still had, it would seem, she admitted even more reluctantly. The way she responded to him was a weakness, some fatal flaw in her character. To respond to a man she despised—it was sick! she concluded miserably. This latest encounter, the vivid memory of the first time—the two had blended together in her mind, left her feeling betrayed.

And she wasn't ready to face that feeling, she acknowledged; she had to do *something*—something to drive the memories from her mind, something to distance herself from Reid's presence and his hold on her... She'd go back to the church, she decided, wondering why she hadn't thought of that sooner. If Reid hadn't been here to distract and confuse her, the church would have been uppermost in her mind. The church was exciting, the possibilities nearly endless... Stick to what you know and like best! she advised herself, grabbing her notebook as she left her room.

CHAPTER FIVE

IN THE gloom, the soot and the damp chill of the gallery storeroom, Kathy had found plenty that she and Reid had overlooked—a veritable treasure, in fact. Now, waiting for this evening's meeting to start, she couldn't wait to tell everyone what was there—the old wood interior window shutters, an assortment of brass hinges, latches and keys, even the remains of the old pulpit and the stairs which had led to it—complete, she guessed, although they had been badly treated and now lay in pieces. There were old memorial plaques, some of slate and others of marble, a few old drawings, framed behind glass; a couple of old wooden armchairs—older, she thought, than this building; a small wooden table...

A gold mine, she told herself, sipping coffee and making small talk, happier now and feeling more human after shedding her filthy clothes for a bath. Even better was the fact that Reid had not yet put in an appearance. In fact, she had seen nothing of him since that bitter exchange in the front hallway. 'Jet lag,' Aunt Margaret had explained as she and Kathy rushed through the simple supper Emma had prepared. 'He's always coming from somewhere so far away—one of those African countries nobody's ever heard of—and the jet lag catches up with him sooner or later.'

Good! Kathy had told herself, grateful for Reid's absence. It was only when Father Gardiner called the meeting to order and began his brief prayer that she realised that her reprieve had ended.

She had developed—or perhaps always had possessed—a sixth sense about Reid. She knew, even without looking, when he slipped into the room, could feel his silvery gaze on her. Blast! she thought, staring blindly down at her notebook while Father Gardiner asked for divine guidance in their deliberations. He added an 'amen', almost as an afterthought, then gently suggested, 'Perhaps Reid and Kathy would tell us what they learned from their inspection.'

'The structure is in excellent shape,' Reid began instantly—not giving Kathy a chance, she noted, inwardly fuming. He gave a complete report on the building's structural damage, emphasised all its strengths—his recital very detailed, very professional.

'Please understand that I can't vouch for the architectural merits of the building,' Reid concluded smoothly. 'That's—Miss Loring's department...' Always that pause, the implied threat that he would say something revealing, Kathy noted, gritting her teeth. 'What I can tell you is that the church was definitely built for the ages. It may be pushing two hundred years old, but it's going strong. You could pull it down—absent any objections Miss Loring might have—but I think that would be a terrible waste. Anything put up in its place won't be as well built, so why not hang on to what you have?'

There was a general murmur of approval—a chorus Mr Blunt didn't join, Kathy saw; nor did she. She was too angry with Reid; he'd stolen her thunder. She'd be preaching to the converted now that Reid had done the job for her!

Still, she tried. She told them about the treasure trove in the gallery-turned-storeroom, she explained the significance of the building, and had embarked on a short history of ecclesiastical architecture when Reid interrupted.

'Don't you think,' he began mildly enough, and Kathy guessed that she alone could hear the steel beneath his words, 'that our time could be better spent planning what to do next? We need to get everything out of the building—which means recruiting volunteers for a job that may take a few days. We'll need Miss Loring to advise us, to check each item as it comes out of the building. She'll tell you what to keep and what to throw out.'

'But I won't need to do that,' Kathy put in quickly, her protest instinctive. She didn't trust any of Reid's ideas, and she wasn't about to let him dictate what she would do. 'Just at first, until you know exactly what you have, you ought to save everything.'

'Everything? Even waterlogged hymnals and prayer books, kneeling cushions, last week's pew leaflets?' Reid enquired with maddeningly detached logic. 'There's no point in keeping every last thing, but you didn't want any good stuff thrown out.'

'But——'

'Take the wainscoting, as an example,' Reid continued, overriding her attempt to break in. 'What if it's the original? Should we discard *any* of it—even panels scorched by the fire?'

'That does seem reasonable,' Father Gardiner observed, backed by a general murmur of assent as he appealed directly to Kathy. 'None of us have your knowledge, my dear.'

'Well...' Kathy knew she wasn't going to win this one—not without an unpleasant scene with Reid—and she didn't need to look in his direction to know that he was savouring his victory. 'Yes, of course,' she capitulated, gritting her teeth. 'I'll do what I can, but just tomorrow. After that, I really must get back to work.'

'We're most grateful for whatever time you can give us,' Father Gardiner told her, then moved on to procedural matters before ending the meeting.

As at the end of the previous evening's meeting, Reid and Kathy had the living-room to themselves now—but if he thinks I'm going to say anything to him he's *wrong*! Kathy vowed. She closed her notebook—the one she'd hardly needed, thanks to Reid's high-handed behaviour—with a smart snap, then risked a quick glance in his direction.

He wasn't even looking at her. Instead, he was staring fixedly at some invisible middle distance—at nothing at all, she decided. Obviously, he hadn't yet shaken his jet lag, and fatigue had marked his features—which was no more than he deserved for dashing back from one of those African countries nobody had ever heard of, Kathy thought spitefully. She knew all about Reid's fascination with obscure African countries! Hadn't he used one to distance himself from her, to destroy whatever chance the two of them might have had?

'Goodnight,' she said frostily, forced to break her vow of silence to express at least the tip of the iceberg of her anger.

'Leaving so soon?' he asked pleasantly—shrugging off the jet lag, at least for the moment—as she prepared to stalk past him. 'There are things we need to discuss.'

'There's nothing I need to discuss with *you*,' she snapped, stopping dead in her tracks when she heard his soft laughter, 'and there is *nothing* funny about this!'

'I think there's quite a bit,' he said, leaning back in his chair, his long legs stretched out—effectively blocking her route from the room, she noted, fuming. 'Poor Kath, you're angry with me, when you really ought to be grateful.'

'Grateful?' She managed a laugh of her own. 'Grateful?—after what you just did to me?'

'Because I stopped you from rabbiting on about auditory churches and Christopher Wren? Sweetheart, if I'd let you get into all that, you'd have lost them completely. They didn't come here for a lecture; they wanted answers tonight. Always begin with what people want—that's the first thing you need to learn about handling people.'

'Which is something you know all about, I suppose.'

'More than you do, anyway,' he acknowledged with a quick grin. 'You're the expert on churches, but that wasn't what those people needed tonight. They wanted to know what to do next. Relax, Kathy,' he advised, still smiling. 'Give them a little time and they'll be ready to hear what you're dying to tell them.'

'I am not *dying* to tell them,' she informed him, her anger only barely hidden behind her icy tone.

'Such injured dignity...' he mused—enjoying every minute of her discomfort '...and I wonder why? Is it that you don't like taking advice, or is the problem that you don't like taking it from me?'

'I don't like *anything* about you!'

'Or is there something else going on here?' he continued, ignoring her brief outburst. 'Were you hoping to impress me?'

'Hardly!' She glared at him, her light eyes flashing sparks. 'Impressing you is the last thing in the *world* I'd care about doing!'

'Of course, I should have remembered that.' He nodded, his amusement instantly gone, replaced by an anger as cold as hers, but one somehow more remote. 'Except at the start, you never did care very much about my opinion of you.'

'Can't you leave the past out of this?' she demanded, furious with him for that cheap—and thoroughly inaccurate—shot. 'Must you keep dredging it up?'

'But that's what this whole business is about,' he countered, eyes narrowed as he studied her face. 'It's the past, come back to haunt us.'

'To haunt *you*, perhaps, but not me. *I've* put all that behind me!'

'Yes, I just bet you have,' he agreed, his eyes hard and so cold that she could feel their chill on her skin. 'Otherwise, I don't suppose you could live with your conscience.'

And what about *his* conscience? she wondered, the basic unfairness of his charge leaving her speechless. Besides, it was pointless to argue; he wouldn't listen... he never had! Cautiously she edged round his feet, fled to the sanctuary of her room.

'Oh, that's a long story.' Father Gardiner stirred uncomfortably in his chair. 'The premium was due—and it's shockingly large, because of the age of the church, and the fact that it's a wooden structure—right before Christmas, which happened to be just when three of our parishioners were laid off work... a cruel and heartless bit of timing, if you ask me, but there you have it—a plant owner who cares more for his profits than the well-being of his employees——'

'That's the way one has to do business,' Reid suggested gently, 'if one wishes to stay solvent, that is.'

'Yes, I know, but you'd think he might have held off for a couple of weeks,' Father Gardiner countered almost indignantly. 'Suddenly I had three families who had been counting on those couple of weeks' worth of paycheques to do Christmas for their families... three families with young children, and nothing for Christmas! Well, I couldn't let that happen, could I?'

'Of course not,' Kathy seconded warmly. Reid might talk about the way one had to do business—that was the way his mind worked, all profit motive and no heart at all!—but she saw things differently! 'You had no choice, but I suppose that's where the insurance premium went?'

'Much of it, anyway,' Father Gardiner acknowledged, 'although I didn't intend to not pay it at all. I was counting on the Christmas plate offering—always a good sum—to make up the difference, but then...' he sighed deeply '...after Christmas, there was a terrible cold spell, and the cost of home-heating oil had gone up, and there were people who simply didn't have the money to pay their bills——'

'And, little by little, it all got spent,' Reid completed for him.

'Yes, but I didn't know that—not for several months,' Father Gardiner explained unhappily. 'I was concerned—in fact greatly distressed—that we had to pay the insurance bill, which meant that there wasn't the money to help as I would have liked, and Mrs Theroux—

she's the church treasurer—told me that she'd found a mistake in her maths, that we had a great deal more than she'd thought, enough for the insurance *and* the heating bills that needed paying.'

'Which must have seemed like a miracle,' Reid offered, a glint of amusement lurking in the depth of his eyes.

'Oh, it did,' Father Gardiner agreed artlessly. 'I was delighted, and quite happily spent all the money, without the least idea that poor Mrs Theroux had decided to let the insurance lapse—just for this one year. It wasn't until the summer, when she was off on vacation, that I found the whole clump of "past due" notices in her desk...and by that time it was too late. The money was spent, and there was no way to make it up.

'So here I am,' he soldiered on, painfully honest, 'with a church to rebuild, and absolutely no money to do it with—which wouldn't be the world's greatest problem, if I only knew how to proceed. There have been donations—an astounding number, in fact. People—even strangers who read about the fire—have been very generous...

'So you see——' he paused to draw a deep breath '—we've got the cash we need for materials, and we've got good workers in the parish—carpenters, electricians, plenty of willing hands and strong backs. We can rebuild this church,' he emphatically assured Kathy and Reid, 'if you two will give us the time—give us a few more days now, then the occasional visit as the project proceeds to tell us how to get the job done. The two of you are the key!'

'Don't think—even for a minute—that I'll do this with *you*,' Kathy announced, beginning at the very core of her grievance. She'd been waiting hours—wondering if Emma would ever leave, if Aunt Margaret would ever go to bed—for a chance to be alone with Reid, to have this out with him. There had been plenty of time to develop a reasonable, rational argument; in fact, Kathy had done exactly that: honing her logic, even polishing it to a high gloss. She'd had a brilliant presentation ready, but now that she'd finally—*finally*!—cornered him in the kitchen, she was too angry to remember a blessed word of what she'd planned to say. The only thing that mattered now was that he understand. 'There's no need of it—you know there isn't,' she continued, glaring at him from the kitchen doorway, 'and I *won't* work with you!'

'No?' he enquired mildly, even as he continued with his task: adding water to the kettle, setting it on the stove, lighting the burner. 'You told the good Father you would, promised my aunt... Now you're going to let them down? Let everyone down?'

'I'll do it,' Kathy said through gritted teeth, still glued to the threshold, 'but not with you.'

'Is that so?' He smiled, one eyebrow raised, then turned away to hunt out the jar of instant coffee, then two mugs, two spoons. He measured instant coffee into the mugs. 'But aren't you forgetting?' he finally resumed, turning back to her, leaning with negligent ease against the kitchen counter. 'I gave my word, and I intend to keep it...so how are you going to manage to avoid me?'

'But you don't have to do it—that's just the point,' she countered, perilously close to stamping her foot for emphasis. 'You must have—for all I know you've got *hundreds* of engineers working for you, and there must be one you can send up here to do the work for you. *You* don't have to stay!'

'I said I would.'

'But that's ridiculous! You can't—can't just stay here,' Kathy sputtered, finally advancing into the room, determined to convince him. 'You're too important to be stuck away up here. You run things, don't you?'

'Only when I want to,' he corrected imperturbably. 'That's the beauty of being in charge. It's my company now, and I can do exactly as I please... and right now, Kath——' The kettle's whistle interrupted him; he took it from the stove, splashed water into both the mugs. 'Right now, it pleases me to do this for my aunt.'

'You're just doing it to spite me!'

'No, nothing as machiavellian as that,' he contradicted, advancing towards her, a mug in either hand. 'Perhaps it's just that I want to keep an eye on you.'

'Why?' she demanded bitterly. 'To make sure that I don't run off with Aunt Margaret's silver and the best of her cut glass?'

'Something like that, I suppose...or to see what makes you tick. Here,' he added, thrusting one of the mugs at her. 'You'd better take it. This promises to be a long night.'

'It doesn't need to be,' she countered, refusing to take the mug from him. 'All I want is for you to agree to send someone else up here to do the engineering work.'

'Sorry, Kath,' he began—nothing apologetic in his tone, she noted bitterly, nothing apologetic in the quick smile he gave her—'but you're stuck with me.'

'Damn you!'

'Unless, of course,' he continued consideringly, ignoring her brief outburst, '*you* back out.'

'Is that what this is all about? Are you trying to make me quit?'

'It's a thought. After all, there's nothing to keep you here.'

'Except *my* promise to Aunt Margaret,' Kathy reminded him, 'and I'm not going to let her down!'

'How incredibly noble,' Reid observed, 'but I don't see why. It's not as though she's anything to you.'

'I owe her! She was kind to me when—she's always been kind to me,' Kathy amended hastily; not for anything was she going to go into that time when Aunt Margaret's kindness had been the only warmth and caring in a cold and lonely world. 'I will not let her down.'

'Then you're stuck with me,' he offered with a careless shrug, finally turning away to set down the mug he'd offered her, taking his own sweet time to sip from the other.

Obviously, he wasn't going to budge, she brooded darkly; he wasn't going to stop tormenting her, and she couldn't leave. 'All right, then,' she said coldly, knowing she was trapped, her anger laced through with bitter resignation. 'If I'm stuck with you, I am.'

'Giving up so soon, Kath?' he enquired silkily, still with his back to her. 'I'm surprised.'

'I don't see why, when you've given me no choice,' she flared, then drew a deep and steadying breath. 'There's no point in discussing it any further. I'll work with you,' she informed him, and now she turned away, heading towards the door, 'but I don't have to like it.'

'Nor I,' she heard him agree—almost cheerfully, she thought, 'and I don't suppose dear Malcolm's going to like it any better.'

'Malcolm?' she demanded on a rising note, stopped dead in her tracks. 'Why are you dragging Malcolm into this?'

'Because he's going to be in, pretty quickly—isn't he?' Reid asked reasonably, but still with that cheerful note—almost gloating, Kathy decided, her temper winding up another notch. 'I can't wait for his reaction when you tell him you won't be back tomorrow.'

'Malcolm's reaction is none of your damn business,' Kathy flared, the fact that she'd completely forgotten Malcolm, that it had taken Reid—*Reid* of all people!—to remind her only serving to add fuel to the fire of her anger. 'So that's what this is all about.' Now she did stamp her foot, whirling around to face him again. 'You're trying to come between us!'

'I wonder...' he mused lightly, deriving unholy pleasure from this cat and mouse game. 'Would it be possible to come between you and Malcolm? Would either of you really notice if someone did?'

'If *you* did, I certainly would!'

'Yes, I suppose you would, given the—what did you call it?—the *chemistry* that's between us...and I'd stake my life that there's no chemistry between you and Malcolm. The poor man——' Reid shook his head, pityingly '—doesn't know what he's missing.'

'It's not like that—we don't have that kind of relationship,' Kathy countered stiffly, very much on the defensive, then added—too late, she knew, 'Not that it's any business of yours!'

'I wouldn't say that too often, if I were you,' he advised quietly, nothing about his tone to suggest that he was threatening her—but she knew the threat was there. 'But don't worry, Kath. I won't interfere.'

'You've been interfering since the moment you got here!'

'You think so?' he asked—that damnable phrase! she thought, bracing herself; he used it often, and whenever he did he followed up by saying something she did not want to hear. 'Sweetheart, if I'd really been interfering, you wouldn't have got off so easily.'

'Easily? You think it's *easy* to have you here? *Easy* to have to work with you and be polite? *Easy* to do anything, to...' She faltered, robbed of the power of speech, staring up at him. Without calling attention to the fact, he had somehow contrived to move closer; suddenly, there were only scant inches between them; she could feel his breath stirring her hair, and his eyes... His eyes weren't dark grey any more; now they'd gone silver—a shimmering, glittering silver—and she could feel the scorching heat of his gaze. 'Easy...' she tried to begin again '... to be with you?'

'No, I'm sure that part isn't easy,' he told her, his voice growing deeper, more intimate. 'No easier than it is for me... to be with you. That part isn't easy at all—being with you, wanting you...' He drew her nearer, his hands resting lightly on her hips as he compelled her to close the distance between them. 'God help me,' he murmured, his lips seeking hers. 'I haven't stopped wanting you.'

'But I've stopped wanting you,' she tried to insist, knowing that her resolve was failing, a victim of his cleverness and her need. 'Reid, please,' she began again as his hands moved to span her waist. 'We can't *do* this!'

'Of course we can,' he said on a note of laughter. 'We *are* doing it.'

'But——' it was impossible even to think, she discovered, now that his hands were stealing higher, caressing her, creating an almost unbearable friction, the heat of his hands on her skin '—I want you to stop,' she managed weakly.

'No, you don't.' His lips captured hers, briefly tasting her sweetness before his mouth closed over hers, his kiss deep and assured, commanding her to respond.

And she had no choice, she acknowledged, her body melting against his, her hands gripping his shoulders. He was winning—had won, she knew in the instant before her thoughts scattered away and she gave herself up to the demands of desire. Her world contracted, then expanded—nothing left to her now but sensation. Incited to respond to his kiss, she tasted him, revelling in his quick response.

'Yes... that's right,' he told her, and she gasped when she felt his caress, whisper-light, on the swell of her breast. 'That's right,' he said again as she arched towards him, seeking more of his touch. 'You feel it too, Kath,' he murmured, making a game of the way his lips moved against hers. 'You feel it... don't you?'

'Yes,' she confessed, the heat of his body kindling her answering flame. She ached for him now; he was driving her mad, the cleverness of his touch withholding as much as it gave, always promising more. She had forgotten what this was like, she realised vaguely; she had put it behind her and refused to remember... but now it was back—all of it, all this wild longing...

'You'd better remember it,' he advised, a note of cool amusement in his voice as he read her mind. Without warning, he removed her hands from his shoulders, forcing a degree of distance between them. 'Remember how you feel now—the next time you're with dear Malcolm.'

She wasn't sure which was worse: his words, or the fact that his self-possession was already nearly intact—far more so than hers, damn him! she thought. Still, she had her pride, too, she reminded herself, withdrawing her hands from his grasp. 'What is it, Reid?' she enquired, possessed by the need to wound him, to pay him back for what he'd just done to her. 'Don't tell me you're jealous!'

Briefly elated, she knew that she'd scored; she could tell by the flash of anger in his grey eyes, by the way he set his jaw, a muscle knotting along its keen line. Still, he recovered well, even sounding amused when he spoke. 'Jealous because of you, Kath? Surely you—of all people—know better than that.'

'I *thought* I did,' she agreed evenly, then struck again, 'until this last little scene. Keep trying that sort of thing and I'll know better.' It was as good an exit line as she was likely to get, so she took advantage of it to escape, refusing to pause when she heard *his* parting shot.

'Keep on reacting the way you just did,' he mocked, 'and you won't be the only one who knows better.'

Perhaps that last exchange had taught both of them to be careful, for the next few days were uneventful, Reid seemingly as determined as Kathy to avoid confrontation. They were scrupulously polite to each other when anyone else was around, and—by unspoken consent—they made sure that they were never alone.

'I don't understand Reid's behaviour,' Aunt Margaret fretted one day when she and Kathy were alone in the house. 'I thought the two of you would be working together at least some of the time, but instead... Well, he seems to be doing his best to avoid you, as though he's still angry, or bothered by having to see you.'

And he'd told *her* not to worry Aunt Margaret! Kathy thought indignantly, then set herself to the task of allaying the old lady's concern. 'He's busy with other things—spending a lot of time on the kind of construction details I know nothing about, plus having to keep in touch with things in New York,' she pointed out, referring to the hour or so Reid usually spent each day on the phone.

'Oh, I know he's busy, but still...' Aunt Margaret sighed and shook her head. 'At first, when he agreed to stay on, I thought it might be—well, that is...' She stopped, her cheeks bright pink, then continued, almost defiant, 'Well, I thought perhaps he was staying to be here with you, that he might want to... well, *rekindle* things.'

'I don't think that's likely,' Kathy said gently.

'No, neither do I—not any more,' Aunt Margaret acknowledged with another sigh. 'If he did, he'd spend a little more time with you, instead of always dodging off somewhere... Do you think something's wrong?'

Absolutely, Kathy agreed silently, but she couldn't explain. 'I wouldn't worry about it,' she offered calmly, betraying none of her feelings. 'You'll see—when we have to start working together, things will go very well.' And they would! she vowed silently, because she'd make damn sure that she told Reid how important it was to maintain the pretence—anything to keep Aunt Margaret from fretting! 'But you mustn't get your hopes up about—about us,' she added firmly. 'Reid and I can be friendly enough, but that's as far as it could ever go.'

'Yes, I suppose so,' Aunt Margaret conceded, clearly not satisfied, 'but you seem to have so much more in common than—no, now don't fuss,' she cautioned when she saw that Kathy was about to burst in. 'Don't blame an old lady for wishing . . . and right now I wish that the two of you would spend just a *little* more time together!'

CHAPTER SIX

AUNT MARGARET'S wish came true on Thursday morning, when Reid materialised at precisely the wrong moment.

'I thought I'd go to Bennington this afternoon, take a look at the old church there before I go back to Providence,' Kathy announced over the breakfast she and the older woman were sharing, the two of them alone in the sunny dining-room while Emma bustled about in the kitchen. 'How long should it take me to drive?'

'An hour or so,' Aunt Margaret decided. 'The road's not terribly good, so you'll want to take it slowly.'

'She won't want to take it at all,' Reid announced from the doorway, his gaze fixed on the side window, where he could see Kathy's rusty little sub-compact parked in the drive. 'Not in that, anyway,' he added contemptuously. 'Better let me drive you.'

'That won't be necessary,' Kathy answered evenly, ignoring the bright anticipation in Aunt Margaret's eyes. 'It may not look like much, but it's never let me down.'

'Are you sure of the brakes?' Reid persisted, holding her with the intensity of his silver gaze. 'Some of the hills and curves are bad enough to make your blood run cold.'

Not as cold as *you* make it run, Kathy thought, just as Aunt Margaret said, 'Reid's right, my dear. It's really quite unsafe, unless one is in a really good car... which Reid's is, of course.'

Of course, Kathy acknowledged with a sense of outrage. She'd just been outmanoeuvred, trapped by two experts. She knew what Aunt Margaret hoped this trip would accomplish; what weren't nearly as clear were Reid's motives, and the idea of spending several hours alone with him filled Kathy with an vague and formless feeling of dread.

'This wasn't necessary,' she told him when, in the early afternoon, she found herself sitting stiffly beside him in the enforced intimacy of his black and lethal-appearing Porsche. 'You know perfectly well that I could have got to Bennington on my own.'

'True,' Reid agreed cheerfully, ignoring Kathy's frosty tone, 'but it made my aunt happy, and it was a convenient excuse to spend some time with you. We've hardly seen each other all week.'

'Which is just how I like it,' she snapped, glaring at him, 'and I assume you do too. You certainly made yourself scarce enough,' she added with a hint of reproach. 'Aunt Margaret was beginning to worry.'

'Well, she's not worrying now,' he pointed out reasonably, 'and now we've got a chance for you to catch me up on all you've been doing.'

'What do you care?'

'I won't go so far as to say that I care,' he countered with a brief, knowing smile. 'It's just that I'm still not entirely sure that I ought to trust you. For all I know, you're making plans to walk off with the silver communion plate.'

'Sorry to disappoint you, but it's already locked up in the bank vault,' Kathy informed him through gritted teeth, 'and if you don't believe me, check with Father G. He's got the receipt.'

'Then what have you been doing?' Reid persisted. 'Heaven knows you've been busy enough.'

'I've been finding ways to get this job done,' she explained, her voice without expression as she recited the list of her activities—her work with the volunteers, her efforts to find grants or special donations.

'You never cease to amaze me,' he observed, his tone deceptively silky. 'You're an expert at restoring old churches—and at fund-raising, too, Kath?'

'Not an expert,' she corrected, striving to maintain her composure, 'but I know more about restoring churches than most people do, and I've learned a bit about finding funding.'

'But what's in it for you?'

'The chance to repay Aunt Margaret for some of the kindness she's shown me over the years,' Kathy answered promptly, 'and the chance to be involved in bringing back what may be one of the finest and most authentic examples of New England church architecture.'

'In other words, a boost for your career.'

'Perhaps,' she acknowledged, ignoring the barb in his words, 'although it won't do me a whole lot of good. There's no heavy demand for church restoration, so this work won't bring many commissions to the firm.'

'But think of the prestige.'

'I'm thinking more of the church,' she countered fiercely, finally goaded into reacting. 'Some buildings cry out to be saved, and something that fine shouldn't be lost; it deserves the best possible care and handling!'

'How noble,' he murmured—amused, sceptical, even sarcastic. 'I wouldn't have thought that higher feelings could ever motivate you.'

'No, you'd rather think that they don't, wouldn't you?' she asked bitterly, wondering why she had bothered. He'd created an unshakable image of her in his mind—dark and distorted, the only possible image to reduce his own feelings of guilt—and nothing she said or did was going to change things. 'Do we have to keep talking about this?'

'Not if you'd rather not, and I can see why you'd prefer to drop it,' he came back smoothly, then relented, and for the rest of the trip he permitted light and inconsequential conversation—almost as though they were friends, Kathy mused, almost as though the bitterness and betrayal between them didn't exist.

It was only a temporary state, she reminded herself as Reid parked the car and they got out to admire

Bennington's Old First Church, but it did make the time together more bearable. Perhaps, she reflected, Reid was as tired as she of the constant battles between them; perhaps he, too, had wanted something easier—at least for this one afternoon. What surprised Kathy, though, was that the afternoon wasn't just bearable, wasn't just easier; instead, it was actually pleasant... in a way she couldn't ever remember things between them being pleasant before.

'Impressive,' Reid observed, staring up at the pristine white frame structure. 'Is this what we'll have, when the vinyl siding comes off?'

'More or less,' Kathy agreed absently, studying the façade of a church she'd known only from photographs. 'This church was designed by Fillmore, and I think ours was too. We've got a more graceful steeple, I think... This isn't Fillmore's best exterior——

'—but definitely his best interior,' she continued inside, her voice now a whispered tribute to the hushed serenity of their surroundings, struck dumb as she began to absorb some of the details.

Her first impression was of light and lightness—sunlight reflecting off the white box pews, the woodwork, the columns supporting the galleries. The walls—a quiet blue-grey—softened and balanced the lightness while the rich red of the carpet and pew cushions provided an emphatic foil. The windows were twelve-over-twelve panes of clear glass, imposing some restraint and order on the views they framed.

'Incredible,' she whispered, stunned by the glorious peace and grace of their surroundings. 'It's almost too much.'

'Too much?' Reid repeated, watching her face with a quizzical smile. 'How can there be too much beauty?'

'But this is almost enough to break your heart...which is silly,' she added quickly, catching herself before she became too fanciful, gave too much away. She bent her head, rummaged through her tote bag for her camera, briskly all business again. 'I need photographs,' she explained, checking the lens setting, taking aim. 'I haven't yet found any records to tell who designed our church, but with photographs I might be able to see enough similarities...'

'Like what?' Reid asked, leaning negligently against the back of a pew, watching her work. 'The woodwork or the windows?'

'Or the dome in the ceiling and the groined arches. I've got great hopes of a dome—those rafters we looked at, the first time we went inside the church——'

'When you nearly went through the floor?' Reid broke in to enquire. 'When I——'

'—nearly pulled my arm out of the socket,' Kathy supplied instantly—anything to keep him from saying what else had happened that morning!—and caught his quick, knowing grin. 'I thought, when I saw the rafters,' she continued with dogged intent, determined not to let him get a word in, 'that they looked different from what I'm used to seeing, as though the church might have been designed to hold a shallow dome.'

'Which would make it one of Fillmore's churches?' Reid asked evenly, the grin gone.

'Would at least make it more likely,' Kathy agreed, relaxing now that this one awkward moment had passed.

It hasn't exactly been Reid's kind of day, Kathy found herself reflecting later—not that you really know what Reid's kind of day is! We never had days like this; in the islands, we had all those sunlit days and starry nights—all discovery and freedom and pleasure—and then... She stopped herself, her thoughts skittering away from those unhappy memories.

The fact was, though, that there never had been a day like this one: Reid patiently waiting for her, taking an interest in what she was doing, making the occasional comment, but otherwise leaving her to her work... *her work*! Kathy repeated to herself with a touch of both pride and disbelief. Eight years ago, she'd had no work, no great interests—except Reid himself, she acknowledged, uncomfortable with the realisation of what a child, a nonentity, an absolute cipher she'd been. In fact, she reflected, she'd been a blank page for Reid to write on, and he'd done just that; written boldly and almost indelibly...

But not quite! she assured herself, and today was living proof of that fact, wasn't it? After she'd finished her survey of the church, he had obligingly driven her to the Bennington museum to inspect a display of some original items from the church. Then he'd made himself scarce while she'd used the museum's library to look through books which described the church.

'I'm sorry,' she apologised when she finally rejoined him. While she'd been working, she'd completely forgotten the time. Only now did she realise just how dark it was, twilight fading into night, the first stars already visible in the clear sky. 'I didn't mean to keep you waiting so long.'

'No problem. I explored the museum—you ought to go back some time, to see the Grandma Moses paintings——' he paused for the time it took them to get into the Porsche '—then reconnoitered and found us a place for dinner.'

Was dinner a good idea? Kathy wondered, instantly cautious. The afternoon had gone surprisingly well, but dinner, she thought, might be carrying things too far. It would be better—safer!—to end this enforced togetherness before something went wrong, so she desperately grabbed for the nearest straw. 'Won't Aunt Margaret be expecting us?'

'I told her we'd be late,' Reid explained imperturbably, a long, angular shadow in the close confines of the car. 'Relax, Kath—after all, it's only dinner. Can't we forget the past long enough to have a meal together?'

Perhaps he could—in fact, she *knew* he could! she brooded as he started the car and pulled out of the museum's car park—but she wasn't nearly as sure of her own powers of concentration.

'Eight years...' Reid mused, then paused to sip his coffee while Kathy tensed. After a surprisingly pleasant meal, it seemed that there was about to be a return to the past, to anger and recriminations. 'Eight years ago, did you ever, in your wildest imaginings, expect to be here today?'

Unfair! she silently railed, nervously fingering the rim of her cup. He wasn't supposed to bring up the past, not when he was the one who had suggested that they forget it for this evening!

For a while, she'd believed him, because—until now—he'd gone out of his way to allay her fears. He'd obviously chosen this place—a wonderful period stone railway station which had been carefully adapted to house an excellent restaurant—with the intent of pleasing her. Until now, he'd made her suspicions and forebodings seem foolish, keeping the conversation deliberately easy—no tension, no hostility. Now, she supposed, he was about to take the offensive—unless she could do something to prevent it.

'Here?' she repeated with a pointed glance around the room, choosing to take him literally. 'How could I, when I didn't even know this place existed? It's very nice, though.'

'I thought it might appeal to you—something old given a new lease on life, something preserved and restored.'

'Yes,' she agreed, still wary, still feeling her way, 'they've done an excellent job.'

'The sort of thing you might do, I imagine.'

Good, she thought; they were back in the present again, and with luck she'd keep him there. 'Not really, because I'm not a designer, and I wouldn't know how to design a restaurant for this space. Research is my thing. I could have come in and told them what was original—like the panelling on the ceiling—and what they should do to restore it, and I'd have advised them as to what reproductions would be most in keeping with the style and period of the building. All I could have done here is make it a train station again—that's my limitation.'

'Still, that's more than most people can do,' he observed, his silvery gaze fixed on her. 'How did you get into the field in the first place?'

'By default, mostly. When I decided——' she stopped herself, searching for a better way to begin, finding none '—to leave,' she continued uncomfortably, 'Aunt Margaret suggested that I might like Providence. She had a friend there willing to give me house space while I got some minimal formal schooling—my high school equivalency—and then a secretarial course. Then, just as I finished, Malcolm's firm advertised for a typist, and I got the job.'

'Then what?' Reid persisted. 'How did you get out of that rut, move into what you do now?'

'I learned on the job, for a while, and then I began to take courses in the field.'

And so much for that, she thought when the waiter interrupted to present the bill; we made it through dinner without a fight!

'You see?' Reid enquired with a quick smile. 'I said we could do it.'

They had, thanks to him, Kathy mused, watching as he glanced carelessly at the bill, then produced his wallet to place several notes on the table, but how had he managed to read her mind? After so many years apart, were they still that close? she wondered, confused by a sudden quick surge of feeling—wariness mixed with hope. Don't be a fool! she told herself, her face carefully without expression as Reid guided her out into the piercing cold winter darkness. Don't hope for what you can't have—don't even want!—she lectured silently; it's better—and safer!—to keep up your guard.

But hard to do, she discovered once they were under way. She could think of nothing to say, and Reid seemed disposed not to talk now; the silence between them unnerved her—but not because it was fraught with unspoken tension. On the contrary, Kathy thought; this was the worst possible kind of silence—an easy, companionable one, nothing but the steady, throaty sound of the Porsche's engine, lulling her into a false sense of security.

In this silent darkness, she was too aware of his presence; it was hard not to study his profile, to watch the play of light and shadow on his strong features each time the car met another, hard not to notice his hand each time he reached for the gear-shift, hard not to think about his shoulder, and how good it would feel to rest her head there...

'What about churches?' Unexpectedly, miles down the narrow and twisting road, Reid spoke out of the darkness, recalling her to the present as he picked up the thread of their previous conversation. 'How did they get to be your speciality?'

'Another case of default,' she explained, steadied by this return to the commonplace details of her life. 'No one else likes them. Work on a church can be frustrating, because you're dealing with a large group of people. It's not like a house, where you're handling just a husband and wife, or a business, which usually has one person in charge. With a church, you sometimes have to try to please the whole parish, and it can take what seems like forever to make everyone happy.'

'And you like that?'

'Yes. Don't ask me why...' She shrugged. 'There's a friendly feeling about it, something to be a part of, for a while, before I move on.'

'Like an island?' Reid suggested softly. 'Something like the way you grew up?'

'I suppose,' she acknowledged, struck by the idea. 'I hadn't thought of it that way...but you're probably right.'

'You're still a transient,' he supplied lightly. 'Still just passing through.'

'What of it?' she asked sharply, forgetting how hard she'd been trying to keep away from hostility and recrimination.

'That wasn't intended as a criticism, Kath,' he objected mildly enough. 'It was merely an observation, an attempt to figure out what makes you tick.'

'Something you've been trying to do since you got here——'

'—and without much success,' he finished for her. 'You're a puzzlement, Kathy. I can't figure you out.'

'Why try? It can't possibly matter now.'

'But it does,' he said, his words clipped. 'Call it vanity, if you like, but I've never stopped wondering what was driving you.'

'Nothing was driving me,' she countered, although she knew that wasn't strictly the truth. At the start, she'd been driven by her love for him—if love was the right word, which she suddenly doubted. How could she have loved him when she'd hardly known him? That wild longing hadn't been love; it had been—what?—awareness, attraction, desire, physical need... a whole dreary set of emotions, none of them anything to view with pride. 'I...' She paused, feeling her way into a new kind of truth, a partial concession. It was madness, she supposed—it had to be madness!—and yet there was something left in her of that quick moment of hope she'd felt when they were leaving the restaurant. It was hard not to think of what might have been, hard not to wish that it might be again... and if it could be—if there was even the slightest chance—then it had to begin with the truth. 'I—I suppose I was looking for something, but I'm not sure what it was.'

'You were too young to know,' he suggested evenly, criticism edited out of his tone. 'Too young, I suppose, to settle down.'

Don't blame it all on my youth! she thought mutinously. Even without that, the relationship probably wouldn't have worked, not when he—— But that was ancient history, the one set of memories she'd promised herself she'd never confront. 'Well, whatever,' she agreed vaguely—anything to get off this subject! 'Nothing went right, did it?'

'Nothing saved us—I'll grant you that much,' he acknowledged, the headlights illuminating a wide swath of high snow banks when he pulled into a lay-by at the side of the empty road, 'but there was something working between us—you can't deny that.'

'Nothing that counted,' she told him, instantly on her guard. It didn't take a genius IQ to figure out what he had in mind now, but she wasn't about to let anything happen, she vowed, determinedly staring down at her hands, which were tightly clasped in her lap. 'Nothing that mattered.'

'You think so?' he asked, out of the darkness, his fingers cool on the heated colour staining her cheek when he forced her to face him again. 'You think this didn't matter, this attraction between us?' he continued, his tone deeper now, a seductive murmur threatening her defences. 'You think how we felt—how we still feel—doesn't matter?'

'It was never enough,' she tried to insist, but the words came out weakly—that damnable, irrational, bitter-sweet hope stirring again—and her voice was a faint breathlessness in the darkness. 'It still isn't.'

'Not enough to keep us together, perhaps,' he allowed, spreading his fingers, threading them through her hair, compelling her closer, 'but enough to draw us together...' His lips met hers briefly, withdrew, then returned to linger longer, teasing lightly at hers when he spoke again. 'And what we had—*this*—was fantastic. You can't deny it.'

No, she couldn't—not now, with his lips still moving on hers. 'But still,' she attempted, using the last of her common sense and rational being to turn away from his kiss, 'there's no point. It wouldn't *mean* anything!'

'It doesn't need to mean anything,' he objected carelessly, his lips finding her temple, her cheek, the incredibly sensitive spot by her ear. 'That's the beauty of it. We're no starry-eyed romantics...' He paused, his lips descending to again capture hers. This time, his kiss was slow and deliberate, an endless moment of exquisite sensation. First came discovery, then increasing familiarity—his lips moving on hers with a sensuous, heart-stopping friction until he sensed her half-willing and helpless response. Only then, when her lips had parted beneath the pressure of his, did he take possession of her, kissing her deeply, guiding her into the dark mystery of her need and his own.

'That's right,' he told her when she reached ineffectually for him, finally drawing her into the warmth of his embrace, into the intensity of pure sensation—what she supposed she'd been wanting from the start. 'There's no point in trying to fight this.'

She knew that, knew she was already lost; she had no choice but to give herself up to the cleverness of his assault. She felt his caress, revelled in his slow journey of exploration. Her breath caught when he slipped his hands inside her sweater; she couldn't help her soft cry of pleasure when she felt his touch, feather-light, on her breast.

'Oh, yes,' she breathed, pressing closer, moving restlessly to grip his shoulders, to smooth one hand along the keen line of his jaw. She fumbled impatiently with his shirt buttons until her palm found the heat of his skin, against the strong beat of his heart.

'That's right,' he said again, and vaguely, as though from a great distance, she recognised the mocking note in his voice. This was no fresh beginning, she despaired. This was nothing more than physical need—the game *he* was playing, and now that he knew he'd won her defeat amused him. Damn him! she thought, hating him for playing the game, hating herself even more for being incapable of resistance when his lips found the pulse point at the base of her throat. 'You see?' he continued, still mocking her when she arched towards him, her fingers tangling in his hair as she instinctively sought to draw him closer. 'It's always been like this for us—hasn't it, Kath?'

'Yes,' she admitted helplessly, caught fast in the spiralling coil of desire. 'Yes,' she said again, her pride in tatters, her only consolation the fact that his breathing was nearly as ragged as hers when he caressed the curve of her breast.

'It's not going to change, Kath,' he told her—promised her? *Warned* her? she wondered distractedly, pierced by the fire of his touch on her breast. 'It's always been like this, and always will be...but not now, I think.' Suddenly, he was gone, the moment ended. He had withdrawn himself, moved back into his own seat; she was left, lost and alone, staring up at him with dazed eyes. 'Not in a Porsche, Kath,' he explained almost gently, in spite of the dry humour in his voice. 'We're consenting adults now; there's no reason to settle for this—for something quick and uncomfortable in a sports car at the side of the road.'

'I see,' she said, trying desperately to strike a cool note as she pulled her sweater back into position. 'What did you have in mind? To nip down the hall to my room every night, after Emma leaves and Aunt Margaret goes to bed?'

'That's right,' he agreed easily—she could hear his smile in the darkness. 'Unless you'd rather—how did you put it?—nip down the hall to *my* room.'

'I'll see you in hell first,' she said through gritted teeth. 'I told you I didn't want this, and I still don't!'

'Kathy...' He shook his head in mock-reproach. 'How can you say that when you were so...eager?'

'You seduced me—you're a positive master at that kind of thing! And that's not a compliment,' she hurried on, forestalling any attempt he might make to have even more fun at her expense. 'It's an insult, but not as big a one as you'll get if you ever—*ever*—try to come to my room.'

'Brave words,' he observed good-humouredly, 'but we both know better. What's between us is too strong to ignore—there's an inevitability about it, and the only difference between us right now is that I'm honest enough to admit it and you haven't quite reached that point.'

'And never will!'

'Never, sweetheart, is a very long time,' he countered softly—a clear warning—then saved her from any further denial when he leaned forward to start the car.

In silence, her anger simmered and stewed. She was furious with him—and with herself—for what had happened. His cleverness and her fatal weakness—the two were a dangerous combination, but she'd known that almost from the start. What was worse about this—this last episode—was that, for a while, she had let herself hope... Fool! she lectured herself; haven't you learned? Years ago, he shattered all your illusions, hurt you enough to last a lifetime, and you should know better! There's no room for hope, no reason to hope. Reid MacAllister killed that, eight years ago—it's just that it took you this long to accept the fact... and let *that* be a lesson to you! she finished grimly, just as the darkness was broken by the few scattered lights of East Hawley.

It had to be late, Kathy guessed. She'd worked late at the museum, dinner had been a leisurely affair, the drive back had surely spoiled an hour or more, plus the incident at the side of the road must have taken... No matter, she hastily assured herself, refusing even to guess how much time had been consumed—wasted!—by that pointless encounter. Clearly, it was so late that most of the town was already in bed—most of the town, yes, but it didn't look as though Aunt Margaret was, not with light blazing from most of the windows in the house, a strange car parked in the drive.

'Company,' Reid observed as he pulled in, 'with an out of state plate.'

Kathy nodded, staring fixedly at the car. It *can't* be, not *now*...not tonight! she tried to tell herself, then abandoned the attempt. 'It's Malcolm.'

'I thought it might be,' Reid agreed, sounding smug and self-satisfied—taking unholy pleasure in her discomfort, Kathy decided, gritting her teeth. He opened his door, then turned back to her. 'This ought to be interesting—particularly your explanation.'

'What explanation?'

'For starters, why we're so late, and why——' Reid paused, studying her by the dim glow of the Porsche's interior light '—your hair is so delightfully disarranged.'

'It can't be!'

'But it is. Here, let me,' he offered, observing her clumsy efforts to put things right, forcing her to accept the indignity of his careful efforts to smooth her hair back and subdue its disorder. 'There...that's better,' he finally concluded, 'although you still look a bit tousled...and guilty as sin. You're blushing, Kath.'

'That's *your* fault!'

'So you keep trying to tell me,' he allowed with a grin. '*I* don't believe you, but perhaps dear Malcolm will.'

'Oh—damn you!' She turned away, furious, fumbled for the door-handle, then drew a deep and steadying breath. 'Look,' she began again, turning back to appeal to his better instincts—assuming, of course, that he had any, which she doubted. 'Will you at least try to behave like a gentleman while he's here?'

'Don't I always?' he asked innocently, then—in response to her dark glance—added, 'Well, perhaps not with you, but I can't believe dear Malcolm's going to have the same effect on me.'

'Don't be clever,' she snapped, getting out of the car, slamming the door behind her. The situation was hopeless, she knew, and the next hour or so was going to be a disaster—thanks to Reid. It wasn't enough that he'd ruined her life eight years ago; now he wanted to do it all over again. It didn't matter to him how hard she'd worked to establish a comfortable, constructive relationship with Malcolm—who was steady and safe... neither of which Reid was, or ever had been. She sighed, hurrying up the walk, but Reid got to the door first, favouring her with a slow, mocking smile as he permitted her to precede him into the house.

CHAPTER SEVEN

MALCOLM and Aunt Margaret were sitting on opposite sides of the fireplace, Aunt Margaret in her favourite rocking-chair, Malcolm in the wooden armchair—the one Reid had claimed for himself on the night of his arrival. Then, Kathy remembered, he had been such a commanding presence, so much in charge that the wooden armchair had seemed to her more like a throne... but Malcolm was unable to achieve that effect.

He was reasonably good-looking, she supposed—although she'd never stopped to consider the issue before—but his was a muted attractiveness. He was of medium height, with medium brown hair, medium brown eyes, unexceptional features—nothing showy, nothing flashy or particularly memorable about him. Malcolm was... well, average, Kathy conceded, for the first time regretting the fact that he wasn't Reid's physical equal.

She had always appreciated Malcolm's averageness; having been badly burned by a man with splendid physical presence, she knew better than most that average was safer. So why now, she wondered, was she bothered by the very quality she'd always prized? It was hardly Malcolm's fault that he was so average—so *depressingly* average, her treacherous thoughts supplied before she could squelch them. It was the ultimate injustice to hold it against him that he wasn't a commanding presence, she lectured herself, overcompensating for her disloyal thoughts by greeting him almost too enthusiastically.

'Malcolm! I never expected—what a surprise!' She advanced into the room without so much as a glance in Reid's direction. 'If I'd known, I'd never have been so late getting back.'

'My fault, I'm afraid,' Reid interjected smoothly, moving in to stand at Kathy's side—as though the two of them were together, she fumed, choosing to ignore the fact that they had been, all afternoon and evening. 'You see, I insisted that we stay in Bennington for dinner. Then, on the way home—well, I'm afraid that we got too involved . . .' He paused for dramatic emphasis, and Kathy felt her blood run cold while she waited for him to speak the unthinkable. 'Discussing restoration work,' he resumed just as smoothly. 'Kath knows so much, and it's such a fascinating subject anyway, that I got too engrossed and took a wrong turn. We've been lost these last two hours, somewhere in the wilds of the National Forest—heaven knows where. I'm Reid MacAllister,' he finished, advancing on poor Malcolm, hand outstretched, 'and you must be Malcolm.'

'Er—yes,' Malcolm acknowledged, forced to his feet—instantly insignificant beside Reid's greater height and breadth—to shake his hand. 'Malcolm Drurry. I shouldn't wonder that you got lost, if you took the same route I did. There's not much civilisation out there.'

'Almost none,' Reid agreed blandly, favouring Kathy with a sidelong glance. 'And not much civilised behaviour—so Kathy was saying, just a short time ago.'

'I shouldn't wonder,' Malcolm said again, giving her a fond smile completely missing the way her gaze was clashing with Reid's. 'Like myself, she's more accustomed to southern New England, which is—shall we say?—a gentler environment.'

'It is that,' Aunt Margaret volunteered easily, speaking for the first time. Her pale blue eyes had sharpened; she'd caught the silent battle Malcolm had missed, and now she used her considerable skills to defuse the situation. 'That's why Reid drove Kathy into Bennington, because he wasn't convinced her little car could safely make the trip.'

'I shouldn't wonder,' Malcolm said for the third time. It was one of his favourite expressions, Kathy knew, although she hadn't realised until now—until she saw the small smile Reid only barely suppressed—just how often Malcolm threw it into his conversation. 'For more than a year, I've been telling her that she really ought to buy a new one, but thus far I haven't convinced her.'

'Of course new cars are expensive,' Reid put in, all thoughtful and judicious, while Kathy steeled herself, waiting for him to toss the next brick through this plate glass window of an encounter. 'Perhaps she's waiting for a rise.'

'I doubt that,' Malcolm answered complacently, missing completely the fact that Reid was baiting him. 'I pay Kathy very well, and she's a sensible girl when it comes to spending her money, very——'

'For heaven's sake,' Kathy put in, furious with both of them, feeling exploited. 'Would you please stop discussing my finances? They're my business—not yours!'

'I think Kathy's right,' Aunt Margaret observed—more oil on troubled waters—rising to her feet, 'and I think perhaps we're all tired. Certainly Mr Drurry must be, after his long trip...'

'And I fear I've stayed much too long,' he put in smoothly, good breeding—something Reid certainly lacked, Kathy brooded—compelling him to instantly pick up on Aunt Margaret's gentle hint. 'It was exceedingly kind of you to put up with me——'

'Not at all,' Aunt Margaret murmured. 'I've enjoyed it—such an interesting time, and I've learned so much...but after waiting so long for Kathy I'm sure you'd like a few moments alone with her, so I'll say goodnight now.' She stopped, with a pointed look at Reid.

'I'll just see to the fire, save Kathy the bother of making sure it's set for the night,' he announced, making it clear that he wasn't about to give her and Malcolm any privacy.

'And I'll walk out to your car with you,' Kathy improvised quickly when she caught Malcolm's lowering expression. She slipped her arm through his, practically dragging him from the room—anything to prevent another unpleasant exchange! 'It was good of you to come all this way to see me,' she told him, chattering madly to fill the void created by his stiff silence, 'and I'm so sorry—you know how sorry I am!—that I wasn't here. If I'd known you were coming...'

'Yes—well, I hardly thought I needed to call,' Malcolm began, nursing his grievance as he shook off her arm to don his overcoat, then his galoshes. Galoshes, for heaven's sake! Kathy brooded; was Malcolm the only man left who still wore galoshes? 'When I learned that you hadn't returned to Providence—to your work in the office,' Malcolm resumed with a pointed reminder, 'when you didn't come back when you said you would, I assumed you'd be here. Since this business, this church, was so important to you that you'd broken your word, I certainly didn't expect you to be off on a—a pleasure jaunt!'

'It wasn't a pleasure jaunt,' Kathy corrected, shivering as they went out into the clear cold of the night. Funny, she reflected, that she hadn't even noticed the chill when she and Reid had come in, just a few minutes before, but then she'd been angry—too hot and bothered to pay attention to such a minor detail... 'Didn't Aunt Margaret explain? I went into Bennington to see the Old First Church—it's one of Fillmore's, and I think ours is, too—and I needed to photograph some details. Then I went to the Bennington museum—although Aunt Margaret didn't know about that—and spent longer than I'd expected, and then——'

'And then dinner,' Malcolm supplied, his disapproval palpable. 'Although it's beyond me why you should waste your time on that fellow.'

'I wasn't wasting my time—that is, it's just that he drove me to Bennington, because of my car,' Kathy attempted to explain. 'I wasn't really even with him.'

'Except at dinner.'

'Well, yes—but that's because I spent so much time at the museum, and we wouldn't have got home in time——'

'And that fellow had already planned that you'd have dinner out—Mrs Pearson told me that.'

'Well, no one told me,' Kathy countered shortly, then drew a deep and steadying breath, attempting to compose herself. 'Honestly, Malcolm, I didn't know until I was finished at the museum, and it wasn't a plot...not worth an argument.'

'This is not an argument,' Malcolm contradicted, his tone as frosty as the air, 'but the whole thing was an inconvenience. I passed through Bennington this afternoon. Had I known that you were there...well, I might have been spared all this wasted time. We might have been back in Providence by now.'

'We—Providence?' Kathy asked, incredulous. 'I wasn't planning to go back to Providence today.'

'But that's why I came—to take you back. Surely you realised that?' Frowning, he stared at her, clearly puzzled as to why she hadn't already grasped the obvious. 'I finished a day early in Peekskill, and it made perfect sense to come up here and extricate you from this nonsense——'

'Malcolm, this church isn't nonsense!'

'Of course it is,' he contradicted crossly. 'At least it's nonsense for you to be here when I need you in the office. I've a great deal of work to get through in the morning——'

'And I have commitments here.'

'Kathy, this is not a job——'

'But I've taken it on, promised to help!'

'Something you had no right to do! I told you——'

'Malcolm...' She drew another breath, clasping her freezing hands together. How had things managed to go quite so badly wrong? she wondered, forgetting for the moment that there had been several times this week when she would have seized gratefully on Malcolm's obstinate stand—anything to give her an excuse to get away from the prospect of working with Reid. But that was then, she decided without hesitation, and this was now, and she didn't appreciate being ordered around by Malcolm—or *any* man! she added in a last minute attempt at impartiality. 'Malcolm,' she began again, 'I am going to do this job—not as a job for the firm, but as a volunteer. I gave my word and I'm going to keep it!'

'But you do have a job,' he reminded her, clearly irritated. 'You can't indulge in such quixotic gestures when you have a job to think about.'

'But it's slow, right now—you know it is!—and you can easily do without me for a while,' she protested, then played her final trump—the one she'd only just remembered, in the nick of time. 'Besides, I have vacation coming—weeks and weeks of it! I've never taken a day—you *know* I haven't... More than six years with the firm, and I've never taken a single day—and this is important, Malcolm. I'm going to do it!'

There was a long moment of silence, there in the frosty darkness, before Malcolm finally spoke, his words every bit as cold as the night air. 'We'll discuss it tomorrow. There's no point——'

'Tomorrow?' she interrupted to ask. 'I thought you were going back to Providence.'

'I was, until it got so late,' he explained stiffly. 'Then, because you and that fellow have taken her two guestrooms, Mrs Pearson was kind enough to make arrangements for me to stay in a motel about ten miles from here. She assures me that the road isn't bad between here and there, so there'll be no problem. I'll be back in the morning, Kathy, and we'll settle this matter then.'

'Not in the morning...' On top of everything else, Malcolm was going to love what she had to say now! 'I'm not going to be here after seven. I've got to be at the regional high school by——'

He sighed, his patience clearly wearing painfully thin. 'What the devil does a regional high school have to do with a burned-out church?'

'One of the history teachers has agreed to let me recruit a few of her students to do some excavating in the cellar.'

'Excavating? Excavating?' he repeated on a rising note. 'Isn't that carrying things a bit too far?'

'I don't know—I won't know until we've done it, but they've got to replace at least a part of the foundation, and I've managed to get the use of some industrial heaters for——'

'Spare me,' Malcolm murmured, eyes heavenward. 'I've heard entirely too much about this church as it is, and it's damned cold out here. What I want to know is when I'm going to see you again. I've come all this way for nothing——'

'If you'd only called first,' Kathy attempted.

'And now I've got to go back alone,' he continued, having none of her excuses. 'I've got to manage without you—I don't like that one bit!'

'And I don't like it either,' Kathy tried to assure him, 'and I will be back soon. Please, Malcolm?' she coaxed, offering a small olive branch. 'I *am* sorry! I don't like inconveniencing you, but this church is important, and I *am* going to do it. Surely, after all the years I've given——' a blatant bid for some stirring of guilt, she acknowledged, willing to do anything to obtain his consent '—can't you let me do just this one thing?'

'Yes—well, perhaps,' he allowed grudgingly, then unbent enough to offer a smile. 'It's just that I don't like something quite so—so unexpected, and to have my schedule so completely upset...well, it's irritating—surely you can understand that?'

'Of course.' Obediently, she nodded, returning his smile with a sympathetic one of her own, gratified when he took her cold hand in his. 'And I won't be completely out of touch,' she reminded him, prepared now to be generous. 'If things get hectic, or one of the things I usually handle comes up, I'm sure I'll get back for at least a few days.'

'That's more like it; that's my girl!' He nodded, finally satisfied, squeezing her hand. 'I suppose we'll work out the details as we go along, and in the meantime . . . well, just don't let that fellow—MacAllister—turn your head.'

'I—well, no,' she offered awkwardly. 'No, of course not.'

'Good. I can't say I like him, and you are very young, Kathy . . . young and impressionable. I wouldn't like to think that he could steal you away.'

'No,' she said again, feeling cornered, unable to do anything more than repeat herself. 'Of course not.'

'Because the two of us make a pretty good team,' Malcolm stated firmly, then leaned forward, pressing his cold lips to hers.

Kathy stood there, shocked into immobility. It wasn't, she reflected, clear-headed in spite of the lips pressed against hers, that Malcolm had never kissed her. He had, although not very often, but he'd never kissed her when she'd already, in the same evening, been kissed by someone else. Not just kissed but *thoroughly* kissed, she amended, and the trouble was that Malcolm was suffering badly by comparison. Malcolm's kiss . . . well, it wasn't a bit like Reid's kiss; Malcolm's lips were just *there*—on top of hers, but not moving, not doing a blessed thing . . .

'There! I'd say that was settled,' he announced, clearly pleased with himself, when he was done. 'See you soon, my dear.'

She nodded, beyond speech, watching as he got into his car, started the engine and carefully reversed out of the drive. In spite of the cold, she watched, waiting until the car had disappeared down the road before she turned back to the house. When she did, she checked first to see if the lights were still on in the living-room. They weren't, which meant that Reid had already gone up to his room; he wouldn't have witnessed Malcolm's kiss, she assured herself with a cold, frosty sigh of relief.

Shivering, she ran into the house, drawn to the living-room to see what Reid had left her in dying embers. Quite a few, she saw, holding her hands out to the warmth of the fire. She'd stayed out there too long, winning Malcolm's grudging approval; now she was freezing. Her fingers and toes ached with the cold; her lips still bore the imprint of Malcolm's frigid kiss.

The memory of it—those cold lips, inert and lifeless on hers—left her as unmoved as the kiss itself had. Yet, she mused, that last kiss hadn't been so very different from the other kisses she'd shared with Malcolm because—and this was the point, she reflected—she and Malcolm didn't *share* kisses. Malcolm kissed her; she accepted—tolerated? endured?—his kisses. Malcolm was the kisser, she the kissee! she reflected, not entirely successful in suppressing a laugh.

'What's funny?'

Reid's voice—lazy and mildly curious—cut through her like a knife, briefly turning her to stone. Then, collecting her wits, she turned away from the fire to find him on the far side of the room, so deep in the shadows that she hadn't seen him when she'd come into the room. Now she eyed him with active dislike: his long and angular form stretched out on the couch, legs crossed at the ankle, arms crossed behind his head to form a pillow—entirely too much at his ease, damn him!

'*You*!' she spat, furious with herself when the word came out more breathless than angry. 'What are you doing here?'

'Relaxing...enjoying the fire,' he offered slowly, everything about him suggesting that he was half asleep—everything, that was, except his narrowed eyes and the shrewd gaze with which he was regarding her, 'and waiting for you.'

'Why?'

'Oh, call it curiosity.' He shrugged. 'You may think it's none of my business, but I wondered what you intend to do about Malcolm.'

'*Do*?' she repeated with emphasis, barely restraining her anger.

'That's right,' Reid said lazily, then swung his feet to the floor and sat up—nothing sleepy about the quick, fluid movement, the sensation of power carefully held in check. 'Are you simply leading him down the garden path, enjoying a casual little fling? Or is there more to it, I wonder? If it's a real romance, have you bothered to tell him he's kissing a married woman?'

'You were spying on me!'

'Watching,' Reid corrected carelessly. 'And some might think I had every right to. Can you blame a man for wanting to know if his wife is kissing someone else?'

'I'm *not* your wife!'

'You were, last time I checked,' he countered, eyes blazing. 'Or are you going to try telling me that you've managed some kind of hush-hush divorce, so hush-hush that even I don't know about it? Because if you are——' without warning, he was on his feet, advancing on her with furious intent, driving her back against the screen around the fire '—it would be in keeping—marvellously appropriate—if you'd arranged a quickie divorce, one of those island specials.'

'Just like that quickie wedding—that island special—*you* arranged——'

'So you remember! For a moment I thought you'd forgotten that minor detail.'

No, she hadn't forgotten—how could she have?—but she'd tried to put it out of her mind and, for the most part, she'd been successful. And besides... 'It wasn't legal,' she said triumphantly. 'That's why I never bothered with a divorce!'

'A mistake,' he told her, extending his arm to brace himself with his palm resting on the mantelpiece, just inches from her head. 'It was a bona fide service.'

'But it was in Dutch,' she objected, clutching at straws, 'and I didn't understand a single word.'

'Which makes it no less legal——'

'But—but...' she floundered, then tried again. 'You arranged it so quickly; we'd only been on the island a few hours when you came back and told me... and then it all happened so fast——'

'So?'

'Are things that lax on Curaçao? I can't believe that people can arrive and get married just a few hours later! You must have done something...'

'Stretched a point, here and there?' he offered helpfully—except there was nothing helpful about the cold light in his eyes, she noted uneasily, nothing helpful in his harsh expression. 'Greased a few palms? Is that what you think?'

'You must have!'

'Ah, Kath, you know me so well,' he mocked. 'Of course I did.'

'Then it wasn't a legal marriage,' she announced, vindicated, triumphant. 'If you lie about something like that, then the whole thing is a sham! I could prove——'

'Nothing,' he supplied, his gaze taunting her. 'I—fixed things so that no one would ever know... Check any of the papers, if you like. Check them all. Check the log, too. You'll find that we arrived in Curaçao in plenty of time to cover the waiting period, and I can even tell you what hotel you stayed in. If they've still got the register, you'll see just how many nights you were there... The whole thing is iron-clad, Kath. We're as legally married as any two people can be.'

'But why?' she all but wailed. 'Why go to so much trouble?'

'To protect you,' he offered with a cynical smile. 'I was making sure that we stayed married.'

'Really?' she asked, determined to prove—to him and, she supposed, to herself—that she could match him in mocking amusement. 'How incredibly noble.'

'Yes, it was, wasn't it? But not worth the effort... as events proved.'

'Then why didn't you divorce me? You could have, any time in all these years.'

'Because I didn't want to—any more, it appears, than you wanted to divorce me,' he pointed out coolly. 'It seems that we are two of a kind. A marriage—an absent spouse in the background—does offer an advantage, a kind of mental brake on involvement. Things can't get completely out of hand, there can't be a legal commitment, so long as that awkward first marriage still exists.'

'That may have mattered to you—in fact, I'm sure it did,' she shot back with righteous indignation. 'It must have come in handy any number of times, been a sure way to keep your ring from someone's finger—and *hers* from your nose——'

'You're good, Kath,' he observed admiringly. 'That's a marvellous phrase. I like it.'

'I don't give a damn whether you like it or not,' she informed him, refusing to be distracted from her point, 'and we are not two of a kind. Don't think—even for a minute!—that what motivates you motivates me. I have not been going around avoiding entanglements, playing games with people.'

'No?' he asked with a sceptical lift of one eyebrow. 'Then what about Malcolm? It certainly looks as though you're playing a game with his heart, so to speak.'

'That's utter rubbish,' Kathy contradicted with a fine disregard for the truth. 'Malcolm and I work together, and we're dear friends—but that's all!'

'Does Malcolm know that?' Reid enquired with silky menace. 'And do dear friends who work together usually kiss when they part? Although...' he paused consideringly, took the time to study Kathy's face '...you seemed—and I speak from recent experience when I say this—you seemed singularly unmoved by dear Malcolm's kiss. Perhaps something is lacking—chemistry, attraction, the magic of pure passion...' He paused to brush an errant strand of her hair from her burning cheek, then continued complacently, 'Whatever it is that happens between us—and magic's as good a word as any, I think—doesn't happen when Malcolm kisses you...and I'm guessing that you just realised that. Lacking any basis for comparison, you'd thought that Malcolm's kisses were fine. But now that you have had a chance to compare, dear Malcolm suddenly seems pretty flat.'

'I don't have to listen to this,' she managed, outraged.

'Yes, you do,' he corrected, leaning closer, the hard line of his body trapping her against the fire screen. 'It's an ill wind that blows no good, and Malcolm's arrival has accomplished one thing: now you know that he isn't for you.'

'What do you care?' she demanded, forced to look up to meet his silver gaze. 'Or did you need to give your ego a boost?'

'If I did, I'd hardly get it by besting dear Malcolm,' Reid scoffed. 'He may be a paragon of all possible virtues, but he's a poor excuse for a man.'

'Then why?'

'Because you're my wife,' he bit out, his eyes suddenly blazing again, impaling her with their molten intensity, 'and I let no man take what's mine.'

'I am not yours!'

'But you will be,' he threatened, 'before this is over...but not now.' Abruptly, he released her, moving away from the fire, shoving his hands deep in his pockets. 'Relax, Kath; you're safe for tonight. I don't take another man's leavings.'

'I am not...' But she was, wasn't she? With the imprint of Malcolm's cold lips still on hers, she belonged to no one, to neither Malcolm nor Reid—which was just how she liked it, she tried to assure herself as she turned and fled.

In her room, though, she found that she hadn't been able to leave Reid behind. She had escaped from his physical presence, but not, it seemed, from the memories...

She had still been unsure—of herself and of him—on the day they made Curaçao. All morning, as the island had grown larger on the horizon, she had sat in the bow, feeling the uncertainty—the hard knot of fear—building within her. After all, she'd reminded herself, all Reid had promised her was passage to a bigger island. Who could tell if what meant the world to her even mattered to him?

He had found a small uninhabited island, had anchored there to let the long, sunlit days and soft, dreaming nights work their magic. She had given herself to him completely, had made love with him without restraint or inhibition. She, who had never shared her bed with anyone, had grown accustomed to falling asleep in his arms, only to awaken—in the silent hours of darkness or the first blush of dawn—and make love again. She had revelled in her increasing knowledge—learning how, in their loving, to please him in the ways he pleased her. Slowly, surely, she had discovered within herself how to draw him to the same magical, piercing edge of desire and need, how to totally share the endless moment of consummation.

All magic, she'd told herself as Curaçao grew even larger on the horizon; this whole week had been magic for her, but there was no telling what it had meant to him. She had told him, over and over, how much she loved him, had watched him, trying to read something from his purposeful movements and narrowed gaze, but there were no answers to be found. He'd been intent upon the task of guiding the boat into the harbour.

'Wait here,' he told her when he'd completed the formalities of their arrival. 'I've got to go to town, clear up some business.'

'Can't I come with you?' she asked, fighting the hard lump of fear growing larger with each passing moment.

He shook his head. 'Not this time, but I shouldn't be long—just a couple of hours, I think.'

Whatever his business had been, it had taken him more than three hours—three hours of the worst kind of torture for Kathy as each minute dragged painfully, weighed down on her imaginings. What was he doing? she asked herself over and over. Was he arranging things for her, finding her a place to stay, perhaps even a job? Was he tying up all the loose ends she represented, settling things so that he could leave her here and feel that he'd discharged whatever duty he felt he owed her?

What was he doing? *What*——? Her heart stopped when she finally saw him; she waited, unable to breathe as he came aboard.

'It's time to talk,' he announced without expression, catching her hand, urging her down into the dim shadows of the salon, drawing her down beside him on his berth, the two of them side by side. 'There are things to settle.'

'I know.' She nodded, staring down at her hand, the one Reid still held. Remember that! she told herself; when he's gone and you're all alone, remember how your hand looked in his, remember that once you were with him, once you were happy, once... But it was pointless to try to store up memories when memories weren't what she wanted, so she forced herself to ask the only question that mattered. 'Are you leaving me here?'

'I can't—not after what's happened. I was going to look after you,' he told her, an odd twist to his voice. 'I never intended to involve you so deeply.'

'I know,' she nodded, still staring down at her hand in his, afraid to move, to upset the delicate equilibrium of these last few minutes together. 'I'm sorry.'

'*You're* sorry,' he repeated with emphasis, releasing her hand to take her by the shoulders, turning her so that she was forced to face him 'Why should you be sorry? You were the innocent, and I—well, I should have known better.'

He should have known better? she brooded, biting her lip to keep from crying. I was falling in love, and all he can say is that he should have known better? 'That's all right,' she finally managed, determined to preserve her pride, if nothing else. 'I suppose—under the circumstances—it was inevitable... and there's no harm done.'

'Are you sure?' he asked, that same twist back in his voice, an ironic inflexion. 'Hasn't it occurred to you that you might already be pregnant?'

'No, I couldn't be,' she whispered, shivering, feeling a little sick until she drew a deep breath and steadied herself. 'That—it's not likely...' Or was it? she wondered, fighting the first stirrings of panic. She really had no idea, had given no thought to the time of the month, couldn't remember... 'I don't think it's likely,' she told him with a complete disregard for reality. 'I don't see how.'

'Still, it's a chance we don't need to take,' he told her, his tone serious, even grave, his hands still on her shoulders, holding her at arm's length. 'One I prefer not to take... which is why I've been making arrangements for us to get married.'

'Married?' she repeated, then burst into tears. 'Do you mean it?' she managed unsteadily. 'Married?'

'Of course.' Finally, the serious note left his voice, replaced by a fine thread of amusement. 'What else did you think?'

'I don't know.' She shook her head, staring at him in disbelief. 'I thought you were going to leave me here.'

'Idiot child,' he chided, smiling at her confusion. 'Why on earth would I do that when what we've got...' he paused, drawing her into his arms, holding her close, his breath stirring her hair '...what we've got is magic—can't you tell?'

Of course I can tell, she thought, smiling through her tears; I've known that from the start. It was just—not that she'd doubted him, she qualified hastily—it was just that she hadn't been sure...of him, of herself. 'Idiot child', he had called her, and that's what she had been, she had time to acknowledge before his hands began to move on her body and her thoughts scattered away.

'Time to get married,' he'd told her later, when she lay spent and complete in his arms. 'Just an hour or so, while someone says the words, then we'll come back here and make some more magic,' he promised, his words soft in the half-light and shadows, casting a spell over her—so much of a spell that she never thought to wonder what their marriage would *mean*, how their life together would be...

Now, alone in her bedroom, she could see clearly that there had been nothing between them—or nearly nothing—except chemistry...chemistry and the unreal roles each of them had assumed. It had pleased Reid, in those days, to play the part of her protector, and she had been equally pleased to let him guide her and keep her safe. She had been pathetically grateful to him, anxious to do his bidding in all things... A match made in heaven, she told herself now with a derisive smile, or so it had been at the start—until reality had intruded, until Reid had tired of playing protector, had tired of her...

CHAPTER EIGHT

IT HADN'T taken long. Just two nights after their wedding, Reid had dropped his bombshell. First, he had made love to Kathy with a kind of wild—almost driven—intensity, had carried them both to new and unbelievable levels of sensation; then, only after the storm was over, had he told her.

'Has it ever been better?' he'd asked, and when—beyond speech—she'd shaken her head, he'd laughed softly, his breath a caress on her cheek. 'Yes, I thought so too, which is as it should be...the last time here should be the best.'

'The last time where?' she'd asked with lazy disinterest, almost too sleepily satisfied to care. 'The last time on the boat, or the last time in Curaçao?'

'The last time before we go home,' he'd explained casually, his voice a disembodied note in the black silence of the night. 'We're leaving tomorrow, flying to New York.'

'Tomorrow,' she'd repeated, stricken, wavering on that one word. 'We're not staying here?'

'No, we're not staying here, idiot child,' he'd teased. 'We can't stay here forever——'

'But tomorrow?' she'd cried with a sense that her whole world was shifting, so slanted now that she was afraid that she might fall off the edge. 'So soon?'

'Why not?' he'd countered lightly. 'It's the real world, after all, and duty calls...' in the darkness, he found her lips and drank deeply from them '...and I won't mind the duty, not with you to come home to...you, and the magic...'

She had shivered, briefly glimpsing the loneliness she would face—long, empty days without Reid, without the anchor of her existence. 'But what about me?'

'What about you?' he'd mocked, still teasing. 'Idiot child, you're getting your heart's desire. You wanted a bigger island and you wanted to *be* something—remember? You'll be my wife,' he'd pointed out, pausing for a kiss, 'and Manhattan's a bigger island, in everything but size. Don't worry, Kath,' he'd added lightly, not thinking—not even caring—at all about her. 'It's going to be fine.'

It hadn't been fine for her. Her happiness had begun to die at that moment—destroyed by Reid, whose power to hurt her had been there from the start. And still was there, she acknowledged now, alone in Aunt Margaret's guest room. Since Reid had dropped back into her life, there had been no peace for her soul. Some things didn't change. 'But I did,' she said fiercely, into the darkness. 'I'm not the green girl he married! I'm strong now, capable and assured...' Until the next time he touches you, the realist in her pointed out; until the next time he strikes a nerve, touches that core of you which seems not to have changed.

Just in time, Reid bit off a curse—due only to the fact that Father Gardiner was present—when Kathy objected again. 'This is getting ridiculous,' he snapped, his jaw set, his eyes lit with a dangerous glitter. 'Can't you let us get anything done?'

'Of course,' she insisted, refusing to back down, gaining some time while she pretended to study his meticulously precise drafting print. It was no surprise that they were fighting, she conceded, but this constant and very public battle they'd carried on all morning was something different.

More uncomfortable, too, she brooded—at least their surroundings were. It was dismal inside the church—too much soot and the smell of charred wood in the air. Worst of all, though, was the cold, and Kathy thought wistfully of the industrial heaters she'd had to return just a few days before. Without them, it was cold to the bone, so cold that it would be a wonder if this work crew of volunteers got through this day without a few cases of frostbite...or murder, she reflected, thinking of Reid.

And their battles were all his fault, she virtuously assured herself. He was the one who had insisted she be here. She would have been happy to stay out of his way, but he'd had other ideas.

'You'd better work with us today, to make sure we don't damage any of your precious artefacts,' he'd announced first thing in the morning. 'We've got to brace the galleries, the steeple, and the floor under the chancel—using lally columns and building jacks, forcing various bits of timber into place...' He'd paused, nodding when he saw her worried look. 'That's right—we could raise hell with some of your panelling, so you'd better be there.'

He was right, she admitted reluctantly—hating to give him credit for anything—still staring blindly at his print. Once she had discovered a lally column's ability to mark and damage wood, she and Reid had skirmished frequently over the placement of each brace.

'You can't do that! Not there,' had been her almost constant battle cry. *That* was why he'd told her to be there, so why was be being so positively beastly about every one of her objections? She was sick to death of his impatience and condescension, his steady barrage of sarcastic comments and caustic wit!

'Of course I don't want to stop you from doing what must be done,' she began again, very composed now, determined to use cool logic as her weapon, 'but I'm not going to let you destroy that groined arch!'

'I am not going to destroy the damned arch,' he snapped back. 'I'm merely trying to hold up that end of the gallery—so it won't collapse on anyone when we start working in here.'

'But you can't! Not with that,' she all but wailed, pointing an accusing finger at the ugly cast-iron building jack waiting to be hoisted on to the scaffolding already in place. In her mind's eye, she could already see how the jack would gouge into the plaster and laths, could even destroy the graceful arch. 'Can't you——?' She stopped, looking back from the arch to his drawing, not necessity but sheer desperation the mother of invention. 'What if you braced under the gallery, just behind the pillar?'

'Or on both sides of the pillar?' he offered, thinking out loud as, eyes narrowed, he studied the drawing. 'Take the weight here... and here,' he continued to himself, one finger tracing the line, 'and then brace here... It would work,' he finally decided, 'although we'll have to re-rig the scaffolding. If you'd mentioned your precious arch sooner, I could have planned this in advance.'

'So it's my fault?' she demanded, standing her ground, ignoring the glittering anger in his eyes to meet his gaze. 'Why didn't you show me your plans before now?'

'I was busy,' he answered shortly—a lame excuse, in Kathy's opinion. 'All right,' he began again, ignoring her to address the work crew—all of whom had been enthusiastic witnesses to the heated exchange. 'The lady has given the order, and we must obey—which is something I wouldn't consider if she weren't so damned attractive when she's this angry.' To the accompaniment of good-natured laughter, he turned back to Kathy, favouring her with a sardonic smile.

'Satisfied?' she asked caustically, and he shook his head.

'Not...' without warning, he moved, capturing her by the shoulders, something dangerous, even reckless, in his burning gaze '...quite,' he finished, his lips claiming hers, marking her—searing her!—with the brief, scalding brand of his kiss. 'Sorry, but I couldn't resist,' he announced when he was done, and her face flamed when she heard more laughter, even a few whistles and catcalls from the men clustered around them. 'No hard feelings, Kath.'

Outraged, she wrenched herself free, moved a prudent few steps away. No hard feelings? Ha! she seethed, consumed by impotent rage. That kiss was outrageous, unforgivable—and if he thought he could get away with that kind of behaviour he had another think coming!

Wary now, treating him with a new caution, Kathy bided her time, waiting until the scaffolding had been adjusted, the new bracing put in place, and the building jack lumbered into position.

'Yes, that's it,' Reid finally announced. 'Let's break for lunch and a chance to warm up.'

She'd warm him up! Kathy promised herself, hanging back as the men of the work crew began a quick exodus from the church. Once everyone else cleared out of the church, she was going to settle her score!

'Reid,' she began, but he didn't move—didn't hear her, or refused to acknowledge her presence. He was standing with his back to her, hands braced on the rough trestle-table which held his drawings, head bent as he studied them. Come *on*! she urged silently, forced to move closer to him, the only way to avoid getting into a shouting match that might carry across the green. 'Reid,' she began again. 'It's about what just happened, when——'

'When I kissed you,' he supplied helpfully, turning to face her, leaning back against the edge of the table, arms crossed on his chest. 'What's so new and novel about that? I've been kissing you—on and off——'

'But not in front of anyone else!'

'So?' He lifted one eyebrow in silent enquiry. 'You're going to hold it against me when I couldn't help myself? There was something about you——'

'Yes! I'd just won a battle, and you decided to show me—and the men!—that you're the boss!'

'My ego's not that fragile, Kath,' he objected, his eyes lit with laughter, with that same reckless—unguarded?—spark. 'I can handle the odd defeat, and when it comes from you, when you've got an idea that's better than mine... Well, that's something new, isn't it?' he finished more softly.

'I...' She stopped, her throat suddenly tight, her mind busy with his words. Something new? It was that, she was forced to acknowledge. All this morning, they'd been treating each other like—like *equals*? she asked herself, disbelieving. The one thing she and Reid had never been in the past was equals—neither in the heat of the island, nor in the cold days and nights in New York. There had been no room for equality there, no basis for it—not when the gap, the disparity between them had been so pronounced...

'I...' she tried again, but whatever words she might have said caught in her throat.

He smiled, an odd, crooked smile. 'Is that really so hard to believe, Kath?'

'Yes!'

'Exactly...which may explain why I kissed you.'

'But not in front of the others,' she insisted, regaining some of her poise. 'Not in public!'

'No? Why not?'

'I...' She shook her head, trying for a new kind of honesty, one at least as real as Reid's had just been. 'I think,' she began again, nervously twisting her hands, briefly distracted to find how cold they were, 'it's that something public—even a joke—is more than...more than I can handle right now.'

'Why?'

'Because...' Heavens! Her hands were freezing, and Reid's gaze was burning, scorching her with its intensity—fire and ice... 'Because this was never real for me—you and I never were—except in the islands, before we...we got to Curaçao.'

'Before we got married?'

'Or just after. If we'd just had a fling, an affair...if you'd left me there——'

'I couldn't do that.'

'Well, you should have! Everything stopped—everything good!' She shivered, trying to rub some warmth into her hands, then finished on a plaintive note, 'Do we have to settle this now?'

'I suppose not,' he allowed. 'You must be cold. So am I, come to that.'

But his hand, when he took hers, wasn't cold. His touch burned, scorching her as his gaze had. 'Reid...' She snatched her hand away, glanced up in time to see him sway, had only that instant's warning to reach out to break the worst of his fall.

Tangled, they fell; Kathy found herself on her knees, taking Reid's weight with her arms and shoulders. Briefly, she struggled, finally managed to get one hand behind his head, then eased him carefully on to the floor.

Reid—this invincible, all-powerful, always-in-control man!—like *this*? she asked herself, still on her knees, searching his face. Reid, his face without expression, his features blank? And how had she—or anyone else—missed that pale greyness beneath what was left of his African tan? She touched his forehead with the back of her hand, found him on fire, found that her hand came away damp, and was instantly on her feet, running for help.

'It's happened before,' Aunt Margaret explained, her face wan and concerned, when the commotion had ended and they were alone in the house. 'Some kind of recurring fever he picked up in Africa.'

Absently, Kathy nodded, went to stand by the fire, wrapping her arms around herself in an attempt to get warm. This whole thing made no sense—not Reid, not her feelings about him...certainly not this irrational sense that she ought to be with him. Reid might have died any time in these last eight years and she wouldn't even have known . . . unless she'd happened to read something in the papers, or Aunt Margaret had thought to tell her. So why now? In confusion, Kathy shook her head. Why now should she have this mad compulsion to be a dutiful wife, a caring wife, a frightened . . . This has got to stop! she told herself firmly, closing her heart and her mind to the wail of the siren as the ambulance began its tortuous trip down into Bennington; this has nothing to do with *you*!

'Not malaria, not yellow fever . . .' Aunt Margaret was saying now, smoothing one parchment-thin hand over the other. 'Oh, dear, he told me once, but I forget . . . but I can call Gregory!'

Gregory, Kathy reflected as Aunt Margaret went to the phone; Gregory still working for Reid, after all these years? Reid, and now Gregory . . . the past rising up with a vengeance, both her old ghosts—one once the cause, the other the witness to the depth of her misery . . .

'Greg will look after you while I'm away,' Reid had announced one evening, the first she'd known about his plans to abandon her.

Later, she'd realised that he'd tried to prepare her—had tried to explain. He'd talked about the family business and the development projects in Africa and the Far East. He'd said something about a bargain with his father, had tried to tell her about scheduling plans . . . But it had all been so much Greek to her, and she hadn't listened, not really, and certainly hadn't understood that what he had tried to tell her was real! Now, in a burst, she asked what mattered most—'When are you going?', and 'Can't I come with you?'

'The first of the week,' he told her, taking her questions in order, 'and of course you can't come. Where I'll be, at least at the start, will be rough—no decent housing . . . maybe not even safe drinking water. You'd be crazy to come—you'd hate it.'

'Not if we were together!'

'Yes, you would,' he corrected, no room for negotiation in his mind, 'which is why you'll stay here—waiting for me. You will wait for me, won't you?' he teased; then—without letting her answer—he possessed her, making love to her until he subdued her doubts and fears.

His answer to everything—she had already begun to learn that. Reid had known only one way to solve problems between them—by exploiting, to the utmost, the physical ties which bound her to him. Now, though, he added a second weapon to his arsenal—Gregory.

Only to Reid was he 'Greg'. To everyone else, he was the more formal 'Gregory'. He was a few years older than Reid, she learned, and had been functionary in the family firm for several years. He was some kind of assistant, she thought, to Reid's father, the austere and remote Barrett MacAllister, who had passed Gregory on to be useful to Reid when he'd returned to New York and to his father's game plan for making him part of the business.

And part of that game plan, Kathy quickly decided, was Reid's determination—or his father's? she sometimes wondered—that she be placated just enough to keep her from objecting to Reid's long absence. The placating—the looking after—was, of course, Gregory's job, and one he did well.

He made sure that everything about Kathy's lonely existence ran smoothly, that Reid's condo—that large, impersonal penthouse in the sky—functioned well, that the staff came and went, cleaned and cooked, did all that well-trained staff ought to do for a cosseted lady of leisure. Gregory organised small outings for her—thoughtfully planned shopping and sightseeing excursions to fill all the empty hours at her disposal; he made sure that she had enough ready cash to indulge her smallest whim, sympathised when she was lonely, listened patiently to her complaints, searched for new ways for her to occupy her time.

By then, Kathy had already realised that she could expect no help from Reid's parents. His father was a too distant figure, consumed by his work, and Reid's mother... Well, she had made it clear from the start what she thought of her new daughter-in-law.

'You can't mean it,' Mrs MacAllister had said flatly, every well-groomed, carefully coifed and styled inch of her in recoil when Reid had brought Kathy to meet her. Mrs MacAllister had looked only briefly at Kathy—it had taken no time at all to dismiss her new daughter-in-law as beneath consideration. 'Reid, how could you?' she'd asked, with only a faint frown to mar her smooth brow, her features only briefly tightening into an expression of distaste. 'This *child*, a girl from the islands...when I had such hopes for you?'

'But I had other hopes, Mother,' Reid had countered with a cool, knowing smile—this exchange, Kathy had guessed, was not coming as any great surprise, 'and surely my hopes count for more?'

'You don't know what your hopes ought to be,' his mother had said coolly. 'And don't look to me to make something of her. You'll have to do that job yourself.'

'Or leave her just as she is,' Reid had countered, still smiling, 'which is what I prefer.'

It had been more than enough for Kathy then, at the start, when she had thought that everything was going to be simple, that she'd be with Reid—and blissfully happy—for the rest of her life. It was only when Reid announced he was leaving that Kathy realised that she could have used some human kindness and contact.

In time, Aunt Margaret came into her life, came to visit Kathy in the empty penthouse, bringing a fresh air of warmth and kindness, plain speaking and humour. 'Eleanora is furious—with you *and* Reid,' she explained, her faded blue eyes lively with laughter. 'She had such great plans for him—a grand society marriage to someone with the same impeccable social credentials she brought to Reid's father.

'You see, my dear,' she continued, settling in for a good gossip, 'we MacAllisters aren't quite top drawer. We were "in trade" when that meant something—my father and my brother—Reid's grandfather—started the firm, and had to work for a living. Eleanora, of course, came from old money. Her family hadn't had to work at it for years—in a manner of speaking, their hands were much cleaner and smoother than ours... although——' she paused to laugh, the small, dusty chuckle Kathy was already learning to recognise and enjoy '—along with smooth hands, they'd managed to shake off any scrap of emotion or *fire*. Eleanora's a cold, bloodless creature—all good breeding and dead coals—and she wanted someone just like that for Reid—which is, of course, why he married you!' Aunt Margaret paused again, laughed again, and then added, 'You, my dear, are ideal. You'll be the saving of Reid, and I, for one, am delighted!'

So was Kathy. In one afternoon, Aunt Margaret brightened her life, become a friend and ally. She made Kathy realise that she wasn't completely alone in Reid's strange, cold family. Best of all, Kathy gloated, hugging the compliment to her, Aunt Margaret had pronounced her ideal for Reid; she would be the saving of him...when he finally got home, she reminded herself, sobering slightly. She was happier now, but she was still lonely for Reid, wondering when this long absence would end.

It was that loneliness which made Gregory so important. He was her only real link to Reid; in fact, it seemed that Gregory was Reid's only link to the outside world. Through the office, Gregory could use sophisticated communications to carry Reid's messages to her, and hers back to him. Even better, Gregory frequently flew out to see Reid—always on business, of course, but he did carry with him Kathy's long, rambling letters to Reid, the ones in which she poured out all the love and the loneliness in her heart.

'You can't just mail him a letter,' Gregory explained when he first offered to carry her mail. 'It takes weeks to get any mail in, when it doesn't get lost on the way... So any time I'm going out, just pass on what you want him to have.'

So Gregory was the link, but never a friend. At the start, Kathy was too aware that Gregory was Barrett MacAllister's man—a part of the hated plans to keep Reid away from her. Later, when Gregory began delivering small examples of Reid's cruelty, Kathy found herself hating the messenger...

As though those messages had been Gregory's fault! she could tell herself—now that she knew better. She no longer hated Gregory, and if—as a result of Aunt Margaret's call—Gregory came up to Vermont, if he and Kathy happened to meet... well, it would mean nothing to her! The years were passed when Gregory had been the bearer of painful truths. That part of her life, thank goodness, had ended!

'To find you here...I couldn't believe it.' Gregory studied Kathy, assessing her appearance before he continued. 'I've been speaking to Reid every day for nearly a week and he never mentioned... Well, you could have knocked me down with a feather!'

A poor choice of words, she mused; no feather was going to knock Gregory down, not any more. The eight years had made a difference in the man she'd known...made a difference in all of them, but in Gregory most of all.

The eight years showed least on her, she guessed. Her changes had been internal ones: she didn't look so very different on the outside, but the eight years had given her self-confidence, some useful skills, a life of her own. While she'd been growing up, the eight years had been maturing Reid—making him tougher, more powerful, hard and lean... and infinitely more dangerous. Those same years had softened Gregory, blurred the youthful cast of his features and thickened his waistline, slowed him down in strange and indefinable ways. He'd become a middle-aged, middle-management man, too solid—even ponderous—for a feather to make any impression.

He was avidly curious about her presence here, had been since the moment he'd arrived. Even as he'd been giving Aunt Margaret a positive update on Reid's condition, Gregory's mind had been busy with questions, wondering how Kathy had come to be here, wondering *why*.

'Aunt Margaret asked me to come,' she offered into Gregory's silence. 'We've kept in touch, through the years, and when the church burned she knew I could be useful...and—for her—I was prepared to do anything I could.'

'But surely...under the circumstances,' Gregory began slowly, watchful, feeling his way, 'I wouldn't have expected you to—ah—run the risk—of...'

'Of seeing Reid? Aunt Margaret didn't think there *was* any risk.'

'He just came.' Gregory sounded fretful, displeased with an unpredictable, capricious boss. 'He does that sometimes, leaves a project and stops in here on his way back to New York—not that this part of Vermont is on the way back to New York from anywhere he ever is! He just decides to drop in—never tells me in advance, of course—to have a break, and to check on Mrs Pearson.

'But that he should come this time, with you here,' Gregory continued, his tone still aggrieved. 'Well, for you, I can't imagine anything worse!'

'Oh, I'm surviving,' she put in drily. 'After all, we're both adults now, and it is possible to coexist on a reasonably rational level.'

'Well, I don't see how,' Gregory countered shortly. 'After what happened at the end...'

Don't bring that up! she thought, her inward calm finally shaken. She had buried the memory of what had happened and she wasn't about to resurrect it now! There had come a day when she'd been able to put the pain away; since that day, sheer force of will had kept it there, unexamined. That resolve hadn't even been shaken by Reid's sudden reappearance in her life—he had shaken other bits of her resolve, but not that hard core... 'That's over now, Gregory,' she said briskly. 'It happened such a long time ago, and I can assure you that it's no longer an issue.'

'But I don't see how!' Gregory frowned, thinking very hard, Kathy could tell, thinking around the edges of a larger concern. 'Is it something the two of you have—have discussed?'

'Of course not,' she assured him, even managing a laugh. 'If you can ask that, you've got the wrong idea about what's been going on here. There have been enough dying embers to deal with in the church; we certainly haven't been attempting to revive our own!'

'So you say,' he agreed smoothly, but his eyes had narrowed, his mind was still very busy. 'But it's hard to believe. After all, things were never really settled—really *resolved* between you——'

'What? You mean a divorce—the lack of the last bit of paper?' she asked, sounding very worldly, she thought—a false touch, of course, but she liked it. 'Well, I haven't needed that kind of freedom, and I can only assume that Reid hasn't *wanted* it. Surely he's found it useful—the technicality that keeps him out of danger of any real intimacy.'

'But still...' Gregory began again—what would it take, Kathy wondered, to satisfy him? 'You must admit that the whole thing is—peculiar...that the two of you should be here and working together... Why didn't he tell me?'

'I don't know, Gregory.' Kathy shrugged, then stood up. It had been a long day—it would have been a long day even without Reid's crisis and Gregory's presence. Now, suddenly, she was incredibly tired, and not about to let Gregory beat this issue—of such strange importance to him, if none to her—to death. 'If you want to find out, you'd better ask Reid—because I haven't a clue.' Reaching the doorway, she turned to deliver one parting shot. 'Look, don't try to make out that there's something—something *happening* between us, because there isn't,' she announced with fierce conviction. 'I'm sorry that he's sick—I'm human enough to feel that—but I'm *glad* that he won't be around for a while!'

But was she? Kathy soon found herself wondering—a ridiculous thought, an irrational thought...but always there, working its own kind of madness. Of course she was glad that Reid wasn't around! And if things were—well, flat? she asked herself, just a bit dull? That was only to be expected, given all the tension there had been between them. Reid had been dominating her life and consuming her thoughts; it was only natural that she now felt a bit empty, as though something was missing...

Without Reid around, her life had returned to normal. She was busy: working each day in the church, meeting with the various groups of volunteers, studying what had survived of the old church records—just as she'd done the other times she'd worked on a church.

Still, she acknowledged, it wasn't the same. Even if Reid hadn't appeared on the scene, this job would have been different. On the other occasions when she'd worked on a church, she'd been housed in an impersonal motel, never able to feel herself a real member of the parish family. This time, however, she had been drawn into a well-established network of relationships; she was, after all, Aunt Margaret's young friend and house guest, living with her, enjoying the time they spent together.

Yes, life without Reid around was certainly more pleasant, Kathy forced herself to believe, ignoring the niggling little voice inside her head which whispered, 'Dull!' Instead, she reminded herself that Reid wasn't entirely absent from her life, and marvelled at the perverse way history seemed determined to repeat itself.

As in the past, Gregory was serving as messenger. He had taken up residence in what had been Reid's bedroom and daily made the trip to the hospital in Bennington, visited Reid, and returned, carrying messages back and forth.

Nothing, it seemed, had changed—except her own role in this bizarre piece of *déjà vu*. Gregory no longer had to think up ways to help her occupy her time. Now she had a life and a purpose, and the messages Gregory passed on to her were very different.

'What's all this?' she had demanded the day after Reid's collapse, when Gregory had offered her the first collection of papers. Warily, she'd eyed the notes, diagrams and instructions, all in Reid's unmistakably precise and angular hand. I don't believe it! she'd tried to tell herself, although she ought to have known that a jungle fever wouldn't stop Reid completely, or for very long. 'Don't tell me!' She'd lifted her gaze from the papers to face Gregory. 'He's already giving orders?'

'He's already feeling a great deal better,' Gregory hastened to assure her, completely missing the barbed irony in her tone. 'Anxious to be out of there, but hooked up to an intravenous line, so—for the moment, at least——'

'He's stuck there,' Kathy finished for him. 'Gone, but making sure he's not forgotten?' she enquired with another look at the papers Gregory expected her to take.

'He wants to keep the project moving.'

'Sounds good to me,' she said, accepting the papers. 'The sooner we get this job done, the sooner I can get home again—and forget all about him!'

But it wouldn't be that easy, she acknowledged as she studied the papers. There *was* something about those spare diagrams and the uncompromisingly angular script. They delivered a statement of strength and power—that from a man who, only the previous day, had collapsed and crashed to the floor, taking her with him. To regenerate himself quite this quickly suggested the kind of force which would stop at nothing. If that was true—and she knew it was—then what chance did she have against him?

At times like this, the idea of Reid terrified her. He had too much power, the power to make her feel things she'd thought were safely buried; he had the power to kindle in her feelings too powerful to control. She was in so deep, she was forced to admit, that even the sight of his handwritten notes had the power to stir her. That was why, when Gregory finally announced a few days later that Reid was well enough to leave the hospital the next morning, Kathy decided that now was the time for a quick trip back to Providence.

She was taking the coward's way out, Kathy admitted with half her mind, while the other half nursed her battered compact on the long uphills and cautiously applied the brakes when the downhills were too steep, the turns too sharp. She was behaving irrationally—running away from Reid, only postponing the inevitable. Like it or not, she lectured herself, she was going to have to deal with him, cope with his presence in her life again.

But not just yet! She needed some time...a little space, she decided, relieved when the rough hills gave way to a gentler terrain—easier on her poor car, and a sign that she was closer to home, to the civilised and well-ordered world she'd made for herself in Providence. Yes, she needed space, she mused, a little happier now. She needed calm days in the office, the comfort of the normal routine; she needed Malcolm, or so she wanted to believe.

CHAPTER NINE

'DON'T tell me!' When he saw her at her desk, Malcolm stopped, satisfaction and doubt at war in his eyes. 'I suppose it's too much to hope that you're back for good.'

'Afraid so,' she acknowledged meekly, liking Malcolm better than ever, liking him simply because he *was* Malcolm, because he wasn't larger than life, didn't make impossible demands on her feelings, didn't upset the careful and deliberate little world she'd built for herself. 'There's a lot more for me to do, but this seemed a good time for a break.'

'The autocrat has things well in hand, then?' Malcolm asked, a slight edge to his voice. 'I can't say that I thought much of him—he's one of those fellows who enjoys running roughshod over everyone else.'

'Well, yes...' If you only *knew*! Kathy thought with a shiver, then resolutely put the very idea of Reid from her mind. She wasn't here to think about Reid; she was here for a steadying dose of Malcolm. 'But we needn't concern ourselves with him now,' she resumed with composure. 'I'm back, for a few days, so tell me what you want me to do. I'm all yours!'

And she was, she reflected happily, when she'd finished the first of the tasks Malcolm had turned over to her. She belonged to Malcolm—not Reid!—belonged in Malcolm's well-ordered world. She'd forgotten how much she *liked* Malcolm—Reid's fault, of course, but she could forget Reid, for a while.

Normality—that was the key! For a few days, she could spend time with Malcolm, could spend time in her apartment, could spend time with Luce—who announced, as soon as Kathy got home that evening, 'You had a call. Woke me out of a sound sleep this morning to ask—and I quote—"Where the hell is she?" No pleasantries, not even a simple hello, and I—of course—was still three-quarters asleep.'

'Reid,' Kathy said on a note of weary resignation, and Luce nodded.

'Yes. Who *is* he?' she enquired, trailing after Kathy while she dropped her briefcase in the living-room and headed down the corridor to her bedroom. 'He's got a certain rough charm, and one of the sexiest voices I've ever heard, but you're not exactly number one on his hit parade.'

'I know,' Kathy allowed cautiously, wondering exactly what Reid had said—nothing about the past, she devoutly hoped, nothing about the circumstances of their relationship. 'What did he want?'

'In the first place, to give you a piece of his mind,' Luce explained, decoratively draping herself across Kathy's bed, watching her sort through her clothes. 'And to tell me to tell you that you'd damn well better be back there by Saturday morning. He's got a busy day planned, and if you're not there he's going to chop up all your groined arches for kindling... I gather the two of you are working together on your aunt's church?'

'Yes, but she's not really my aunt. She's his.'

'He seemed to think he knew you very well,' Luce mused thoughtfully, head cocked to the side, studying Kathy's apparent nonchalance. 'He said you have a habit of running away, and I said that I wouldn't have pegged you as the type, that—as far as I know—you've been living here for a number of years, but——' she shrugged, watching Kathy through narrowed eyes '—he seemed to feel otherwise.'

'For pity's sake!' Kathy turned, appalled, the colour high in her cheeks. 'The two of you didn't discuss it, did you?'

'Discuss *what*?' Luce demanded, pouncing on Kathy's little slip. 'What's going on between the two of you?'

'Nothing,' Kathy answered lamely, glad that—with a clean pair of jeans and a sweat-shirt in hand—she could turn her back on Luce to change. 'There's no telling what he means—he'll say anything to get his way, and he's probably furious that I came to give Malcolm a hand for a few days.'

'Oh, Malcolm,' Luce said with a snort. 'This man's miles ahead of poor bloodless Malcolm. Is he attractive?'

'I expect you'd think so,' Kathy allowed, her voice muffled as she pulled the sweat-shirt over her head. 'At least——' she turned back, eyeing the lanky Texan sprawled on the bed '—he'd be tall enough for you.'

'And dark and handsome?' Luce prompted hopefully. 'And rich enough to keep a poor struggling student-artist?'

'Richer than sin,' Kathy said, her tone uncharacteristically bitter. 'That's part of his problem—that he's always been able to have what he wants. He's spoiled.'

'I could overlook that,' Luce decided with a quick grin, 'so long as didn't mind spoiling me. Any chance that I'll meet this paragon?'

'None at all,' Kathy announced grimly. Reid was in Vermont, her life was here—and never the twain would meet, she devoutly hoped.

In the meantime, she settled happily into her familiar routine. On Friday she would have to drive back to East Hawley—but not, she hastened to assure herself, because of Reid's phone call! She wasn't jumping when he said to jump; she'd known from the start that she'd have to be there for the weekend, when the volunteers were planning to tackle several large projects.

Malcolm, knowing she was leaving on Friday, took her out for dinner on Thursday evening. It was a pleasant meal of easy, comfortable conversation . . . just what she had needed, Kathy mused silently as they lingered over their coffee. This was an affirmation of the reality of her life, a reminder of what she had never had—and never could have!—with Reid . . .

'Well, I know you're pretty well caught up,' Malcolm began, breaking the companionable silence between them, 'but I wish you weren't leaving quite so soon. Who knows when I'll see you again?'

'Next week—I'll be back after the weekend,' Kathy offered, mentally crossing her fingers, hoping Reid wouldn't prevent her from making good her promise. 'Just give me the weekend—I've got to be there for Saturday's workday, but after that——'

'After that, something else will come up to keep you away,' Malcolm grumbled. 'That man—MacAllister—will think up some new reason to keep you there, and at my expense. It's probably deliberate, simple spite,' he continued, his discontent gathering momentum. 'He wants your undivided attention, wants you working only for him. It's obvious that he dislikes the fact that I have—or rather *had*, until he appeared on the scene—the greater claim to your time.'

If it were only that simple, Kathy brooded, wishing Malcolm would drop the subject. There was so much more to Reid—to the situation between the two of them—than Malcolm could imagine. The fact that he didn't understand was hardly his fault; it couldn't be, when she had told him nothing—nothing that counted, anyway—of her past.

She had only herself to blame. She'd buried her life with Reid, pretending it had never happened, trying to convince herself... She'd have pulled it off, too, if *this* hadn't happened, if the church in East Hawley hadn't burned, if Aunt Margaret hadn't asked for her help, if Reid hadn't arrived on the scene...

All those ifs, Kathy brooded, and Reid's long shadow was casting a pall over this evening, as though there was no escaping him...

No! she wasn't going to think that, she told herself fiercely. This business, the whole nightmare of Reid, was just a temporary matter. As soon as the work was finished, as soon as Reid was out of her life again...

'Things *will* get back to normal,' Kathy said, determined to convince both Malcolm and herself that it was so. 'You'll see—it won't be very long.'

'Still, I don't like it,' Malcolm complained, insisting on his right to have the last word. 'He's trouble—not at all our sort. The man is rude and crude and thoroughly unprincipled, and I don't like the idea of your spending so much time with him.'

Nor did she, Kathy acknowledged silently. She didn't even like the fact that Malcolm was spending so much time talking about him. It was giving her a headache, a tight band of tension pressing in on her, the very thought of Reid ruining her evening.

But the thought of Reid was nothing, when compared to the reality. Impossible and unbelievable, the worst possible... and even worse than that, Kathy told herself when she realised what was happening.

It only took a moment. Outside her door, Malcolm beside her, playing perfect gentleman, Kathy fumbled for her key.

Before she'd found it, Luce had unlocked the door from the other side. Even as she began to swing it open, Kathy heard her say, 'Good thing you didn't invite—— Oh!' She stopped when she saw Malcolm, grinned as she continued, 'Hello, Malcolm... Kathy, you've got another visitor.'

Kathy already knew, had known from the instant she'd seen Reid's tall presence looming behind Luce... She'd been right, Kathy told herself—a random thought while speechlessness still held her in its grip—Reid *was* tall enough for Luce.

'I don't believe it,' Kathy spat when she'd finally found her tongue. 'You *can't* be here!'

'But I am,' he pointed out, stating the painfully obvious as Luce moved aside.

Still grinning, damn her! Kathy noted, before looking back to Reid, struck speechless once again. He was so—

so *large*, she reflected, and so alive! He dwarfed her little hallway and, when he moved forward, hand outstretched in greeting, he dwarfed Malcolm. Reid MacAllister was a hateful man, Kathy brooded, furious with him and with herself for letting him get to her, and then, belatedly, with Malcolm who made an awkward moment even worse by refusing to shake hands.

'Well, Kathy,' he began, avoiding Reid's existence, 'this is not a place I care to be—not with the present company—so I shall say goodnight.'

'Yes—I—of course,' she sputtered, incredulous, willing him to disappear when she realised that he actually intended—and in front of Reid, for pity's sake!—to kiss her. No! she thought, despairing, closing her eyes as Malcolm pressed his lifeless lips to hers, held them there for a moment, then removed them.

'Goodnight, my dear,' he told her, then turned on his heel, his back rigid, bristling with disapproval as he walked back to his car.

'Well, I've been put in my place, haven't I?' Reid observed, laughter in his voice, the whole thing a gigantic joke. 'But no matter... Kath, come inside, so I can close the door.'

'*You*! What are you doing here?' she demanded, but the edge that she'd hoped for wasn't there. Instead there was a slight breathless quality to her voice—thanks, she supposed, to the unexpectedness of his presence; that, and the fact that it had been eight years since she'd seen him in a suit. She had forgotten what was now all too easy to remember: the potent combination of elegance and hard muscularity only partly disguised by fine tailoring. The first time she'd seen him like this—the consummate businessman, setting off for the day at the office—he'd laughed at her sudden shyness, teased her and said... But she would not think of that now; not now, not ever. That was the past; it was over! 'What are you doing here?'

'Waiting for you.' He stated the obvious with a quick grin, wise to her, knowing just what a storm of emotion his appearance had caused.

'I know that,' she countered with a little more poise, her anger a steadying force, 'but why?'

'I had to make a quick trip to New York this morning, and I decided to stop off here on my way back. We can go back to Vermont tomorrow... together.'

'I'm not going with you,' she put in, determined, ignoring Luce's presence, the avid curiosity with which she was following this exchange. 'I'll drive myself.'

'No, you won't,' he corrected with slight emphasis. 'You'd never make it, not in your car. There's been a fair bit of snow, and more forecast for tomorrow night. I'll pick you up here at noon.'

She shook her head, then improvised. 'That's no good. I promised Malcolm I'd work with him until four...' A lie, but it would buy her time, time to start out alone on the trip—anything to avoid having to travel with Reid. 'I can't leave at noon.'

'Too bad. You're going to have to disappoint dear Malcolm.' He started to leave, then paused briefly, eyes narrowed to read her expression, the one she'd hoped was revealing nothing at all. 'And don't even think about skipping out early on me.'

'You can't stop me.'

'True,' he acknowledged with a quick grin, 'but if you try, you'll pay—before this weekend is over. Why not behave, sweetheart?' he suggested. 'It's so much easier all around... and one thing more...' Without warning, he moved in on her, caught her to him, his mouth descending to capture hers, moving surely to exploit all her weaknesses... So clever, so alive! she acknowledged, knowing she couldn't help herself. Already she was responding, her lips parting to admit him, wanting whatever he offered, wanting to give back even more... '*That's* how you ought to be kissed,' Reid finally told her, his lips still just inches from hers. '*Not* the way that poor codfish of a man tries to kiss you! You've got too much spirit for a man like that...'

And suddenly, definitely, he was gone; she heard Luce exclaim, 'Delicious! He's the man for you!'

'He's *not*,' Kathy managed in return. 'I *hate* him! And I will not talk about him, no matter *what* you say!'

'How are you?' Kathy asked when they'd left Providence, the spaghetti strands of the inter-state highway now behind them. 'Feeling better?'

'Just being polite?' he countered with a quick glance, an even quicker smile. 'Or do you really care?'

'I'd prefer that you don't pass out again, at least not until we're on the ground.'

'Heartless girl...'

'A realist,' she corrected carefully. 'I don't know how to fly.'

'And I don't know if you're teasing me or not. Still,' he continued lightly, 'I'm glad you came. Are you?'

'You know I'm not,' she told him, but almost gently, without the anger that so often marked their exchanges. Perhaps she'd mellowed slightly, she reflected, or was it that he'd—at least this time—won a round? Lost in thought, she looked down to watch the passing scene. Now it was more rural—a soothing, muted patchwork landscape of open fields and woods, of brown and black and white and the occasional living colour of a stand of evergreens.

He had won this round—coming to her apartment a good two hours before he'd said he would. He'd caught her almost at the last possible moment, about to load her car and leave... She should have known! she told herself, then wondered if she *had* known, if she'd been playing a game of her own—trying to believe she didn't want to be with him, while making sure she would be. But if that were true...

'It's a mistake,' she told him—and herself. 'We'd both be better off if none of this had happened.'

'None of it?' he questioned, with subtle emphasis. 'There have been some peak experiences—those first days on the boat, the battle over your groined arches...'

Which was not what she'd expected him to say, that he would consider anything about her—now—to be a peak experience... Something else to think about, and she did, while they left the patchwork behind. Now there was nothing below them but forest—a wilderness of bare branches, the occasional evergreens, the glinting silver-grey of a stone bluff.

Then ahead, and soon beneath them, were rolling hills, their random irregularity beginning to form a pattern of gathering height. Within the plane's small cabin, the sound of the motor was suddenly louder as Reid adjusted the controls. The plane seemed to be gaining altitude, climbing higher into the darkening gun-metal-grey sky. She guessed that somewhere, off to the west—her left—and invisible behind the heavy cloud cover, the sun was beginning to set.

The world looked cold and lifeless, she thought with a shiver: one small, spare town in a valley and then nothing but wooded hills, the black angularity of branches against the snow... and snow in the air now, she noted, shivering again.

'Cold?' Reid asked with a quick glance.

She shook her head. 'Just thinking how cold it must be down there. Are we over Vermont yet?'

'Just about,' he answered, just as the motor chose to miss a few beats, to catch again, and then miss a few more.

'What is it?' Kathy asked carefully, her voice hushed. She knew it was silly, but something within her was superstitious, was trying to avoid distracting the motor while it laboured to regain its smooth, consistent note. 'Is something wrong?'

Reid didn't answer. He was fiddling with some of the switches on the instrument panel, his expression intent. He used the radio briefly—so much Greek to her, first the jargon of the call letters, then a few real words which she later guessed she had blocked out of her mind in an attempt to avoid the truth of their situation.

Finally, it seemed, he remembered her presence. 'We've got to land,' he told her without looking at her. Instead, he was peering at the ground, eyes narrowed to pierce through the snow which was now falling faster. 'Look out your side. See if you can find a clearing.'

Without a word, she started to scan the ground, searching for any spot free of the tangle of bare branches or sullen grey rock.

In the end, it was Reid who found a promisingly open stretch in the woods. 'A pond, I think,' he told her, 'and it just might be long enough.'

'Will we crash?'

'Not if I can help it.'

That's good enough for me, she decided as Reid guided the plane in long, downward spirals. Think what she would about him—and she'd thought a lot, and none of it good, she acknowledged—he was the man to have in a crisis. He was competent, very cool, always thinking things through, knowing what had to be done and doing it...

Without question or comment, she followed his instructions to tighten her seatbelt and brace herself, waited, staring blindly at her hands, listening to the motor's final, faltering attempts. In the silence, she heard the wind rushing past the plane, felt the first rough jolt as the landing gear snagged on something—snow, or a tree branch? she had an instant to wonder—and then nothing at all, until Reid's voice pierced the emptiness.

'Kath? Are you all right?'

Was she? She had no idea. For all she knew, she was dead; perhaps they both were—a cosmic joke there, she had the wit to realise: the two of them, stuck with each other for all eternity...

'Are we alive?' she finally managed, and heard the thread of Reid's laughter.

'Of course we are. Take a look.'

She did, focusing on Reid, who appeared to be very much alive. In a world of grey and black and white, he was colour—the brownish-gold remnants of his tan, the reddened gash on his forehead, the bruise beneath already turning an interesting shade of purple.

'I guess we are alive,' she finally managed on a shaky laugh. 'Are you hurt?'

Briefly, he touched his hand to the gash. 'Only this, I think. What about you?'

'I'm not sure.' Cautiously, she checked: moved her arms and her legs, her fingers, her toes, took a deep breath, then shook her head. 'I'm fine.'

'We'll both be sore in the morning.'

He was probably right—not that it mattered. What mattered was that they were alive, that they'd survived a plane crash... 'What do we do now? Wait to be rescued?'

'We won't be rescued today.'

'But you used the radio. You told them where we were, didn't you?'

'Yes, but no one will come looking for us today. It's almost dark, and there's the makings of a blizzard out there.'

'Then do we wait here in the plane?' she asked, determined to be practical, to understand this bizarre twist of fate. 'It's going to get cold.'

'Too cold,' he agreed, the humour gone from his voice now, suddenly as practical as she was trying to be. 'As we came in, I thought I saw a building at the edge of the pond, off there——' he paused, checked the compass on the control panel '—to the south, I think. I'll take a look, and—if I find it—we can wait out the storm there. Otherwise, I'll build a shelter, see if I can get a fire started...' He retrieved his jacket from behind his seat, shrugged into it, hunted the pockets until he found a pair of leather gloves. 'You wait here—there's some warmth left for you—and I'll be back as soon as I can.'

'I'm not going to stay here alone, and you're not going out there alone,' she protested, indignant. 'You might break your leg, or pass out, or——'

'I'll be fine.'

'But I'm not taking chances. You got me into this,' she accused, 'so don't think——' it was her turn to hunt up her jacket, her gloves, the scarf she'd remembered to bring '—not for a minute, that I'm letting you go off alone!'

'Look,' he began reasonably enough, 'I've got to find us some shelter before it gets dark, and you'll slow me down.'

'I won't,' she vowed. Not waiting for his response, she pushed open her door and found herself plunged into a pure misery of cold, the wind-driven snow stinging her face. Gritting her teeth, she set off after Reid, forcing herself to maintain his killing pace through a hostile white world. It helped, she supposed, that he led the way, breaking a faint path across the frozen surface of the pond. Still, she had to take nearly two steps for each one of his long strides, and sometimes she foundered in deep drifts.

Just when she'd begun to believe that their situation was hopeless, when she feared they would never find this mythical structure Reid claimed to have seen from the air, Reid stopped. He turned to watch her, impatiently measuring her slow progress—waiting, she knew, to say, 'I told you so.' Well, she wasn't going to let him! she promised herself, finding a fresh store of energy and pushing on.

'Hang on,' he told her, his words barely audible over the shriek of the storm. 'I can see it—just over there.'

She nodded, beyond words, but she had seen it, too—a dark and rectangular shadow among the more random angles of the trees. Shelter, she thought, and kept repeating the word—once for each step she took—and, with each step, the shadow took on greater substance.

It was a small, weathered cabin, roughly built with a steeply pitched roof, windows boarded over, the door fastened with a stout padlock—and a lot of good it will do us, she brooded, if we can't get in! Standing motionless, the snow at her face and the cold settling in her bones, she watched Reid tackle the lock, using a stout stick to pry the padlock's hasp out of the wood.

'Come on,' he shouted, when he'd worked the door ajar. 'Let's get inside.'

Gladly! she thought, taking his hand, permitting him to thrust her out of the storm and into a quieter darkness. For a moment, she stood alone, alone and disorientated, then Reid was beside her, stamping his feet, blowing fiercely on his hands.

'You see?' he said, sounding pleased with himself, and she felt herself caught up against him, held in an iron grip, felt his breath, warm on her cheek. 'We made it.'

'Yes,' she managed stiffly, her face so cold now that it felt as though it might crack if she tried to smile, 'but only barely.'

'But "barely" counts,' he told her, then went briefly still, staring down at her with a sudden intensity. Then, without warning, the moment passed; he released her and turned away. 'Time to do something about getting warm.'

Warm? Warm was a relative term, Kathy reflected, and the shelter they'd found was pretty minimal—not that she was going to look this particular gift-horse in the mouth. Anything—anything at all! she assured herself with heartfelt fervour—was better than the raging storm outside, and this place had the potential to be a reasonably snug refuge.

First, Reid had found a kerosene lamp which, when lit, provided at least the illusion of warmth—a pale golden-orange light which drove back the shadows and permitted them to inspect their surroundings. 'Not bad,' Reid mused, prowling the one large room. 'We've got a stove and some firewood...a flashlight...canned goods, coffee...'

'Even a privy,' Kathy contributed brightly, opening the door on the far side of the room. A definite afterthought, she noted, a little cubicle tacked on to the main cabin, and so carelessly built that she could feel the cold wind whistling through the many cracks in the walls. She shivered and hurried to push the door shut. 'Not exactly a modern convenience,' she reported to Reid, 'but slightly better than having to go outside when nature calls.'

'Speaking of which——'

'What—nature calling?' she asked on the edge of a laugh.

'No. Going outside,' he explained briefly, checking the flashlight he'd found. 'We'll need more firewood before we're done, and there's a stack out there. Wait here while I bring some in.'

'But...' Ignoring Kathy's attempted objection, Reid slipped through the door, leaving her feeling very much alone, the kerosene lamp a frail defence against the howling wind and icy cold.

Not for long, though. He was back almost immediately, his arms piled high with wood. She watched him drop it to the floor, watched him stamp the snow from his feet, watched wide-eyed, aware of a sudden change in how she felt about him. They had shared something important—those endless, heart-stopping moments in the air when they had known they were in trouble, the miserable trek through the storm before they'd found the relative shelter of this cabin. They'd been through all of that, and he—— 'You saved my life!'

'Don't be an idiot, Kath,' he told her, sounding both kind and faintly amused—a superior being, capable of taking things like this in his stride, she supposed. 'We were never in any real danger.'

'We could have been killed,' she protested, following him to the old cast-iron stove, watching with greedy eyes as he got a fire going. 'If you hadn't been able to land the plane on the ice, or if you hadn't found this place——'

'But we did. We're all right, or will be, when we get some warmth in here.' He straightened up, looking around the room. 'This place is built like a sieve—pity the owner didn't invest in a little insulation. Still——'

'Beggars can't be choosers,' Kathy supplied, earning an ironic smile.

'You're being a remarkably good sport about all of this. I expected recriminations—after all, I got you into this mess.'

'And got me out,' she reminded him, watching as he turned away from the fire and began to prowl the room, finally pulling some clothing down from a hook near the bunk beds.

'Here, put this on,' he told her, thrusting a thick flannel bathrobe into her hands. 'We need to change before the snow melts. Stand by the stove,' he advised, going to feed the fire more wood.

'What about you?'

'I found some jeans and a shirt.'

Was he planning to change now too? she wondered, swallowing against the sudden dryness in her mouth. Was he going to strip out of his wet clothing and stand beside her, the golden light from the kerosene lamp reflecting off his skin, burnishing his hard-muscled strength?

'I don't think...' she began awkwardly, clutching the bathrobe to her like a shield. 'That is...I could change in the privy,' she offered quickly.

'Don't be an idiot, Kath,' he said brusquely—it seemed to have become his favourite expression. 'I won't look, if that's what you're worried about...not that it matters,' he added softly as she moved back to the stove, elaborately turning away from him before starting to change. 'Remember? I've seen it all, plenty of times.'

'That was then,' she countered tightly, fumbling with her clothing, alive to the sounds of him changing behind her. 'And you're *not* going to see it now!'

'It's of no concern to me,' he told her, all the warmth instantly gone from his voice, once again very cool, very self-possessed. 'Warmth is all that counts right now.'

Damn the man, she fumed, tripping over the hem of the bathrobe in her attempts to help him put a simple meal together from the canned goods on the shelf. He had more to do with keeping her off-balance than the stupid bathrobe. He was being too—too changeable, she concluded peevishly. He was showing too many sides of himself, confusing her, leaving her uncertain. Once more, she tripped over the hem, cursed, and heard his quick laughter.

'Give it up, Kath,' he advised. 'You're a positive menace when you walk. Go sit down and let me put the meal together.' He put down the can opener to steer her towards the chair closest to the stove.

Strange, she brooded, watching him move around the shadowy room, opening cans, finding a cooking pot. How could things seem so perfectly *normal* when the situation was so bizarre? Turning inward to follow her thoughts, she tried to work out why it was that everything seemed so familiar—so like the best of times, she realised, leaning a little closer to the fire.

Tonight was too much like the best of times, this evening too much like those other evenings, on the boat. Strange to believe—that this cold and howling night in this rough cabin could be in any way like those soft, warm evenings on the boat—but it was true. It was the intimacy, the aloneness of the two of them, the softly glowing light... Those times had spun a tangled web of emotion, binding her to him...and nothing, she realised, sitting up a little straighter, had destroyed those feelings. They were as real as they had ever been, fresh and alive in her, and Reid suddenly too much like the man he'd been eight years ago.

That was what had caught her so terribly off-balance: the absence of his hard edge. Since the night he'd materialised in Aunt Margaret's living-room, there had always been about him an ominous, threatening anger, a taunting ability to provoke. She really hadn't seen the old Reid—the first Reid, the one she'd loved so deeply—until tonight. Now that she had, she shivered yet again, frightened, understanding just how vulnerable she was. There was danger for her here, alone with Reid, perhaps not tonight, but—if this enforced togetherness went on much longer—very soon.

'How long do you think we'll be here?' she asked, abandoning the small talk when they had finished their meal.

'Hard to say,' Reid offered easily, getting up to pour more coffee into her mug and his own. 'A lot depends on the storm—no one's going anywhere until it ends.' He resumed his place at the table, tilted his chair back to a comfortable angle and took a sip of his coffee. 'After that, a lot depends on where we are.'

'You don't know where we are?'

He shrugged. 'Not exactly. Somewhere near the state line—north-western Massachusetts or southern Vermont.'

'But...' She paused, fighting a sudden sense of panic. If he didn't know where they were, how would anyone else? And if no one knew, how long would it be until a search party found them? How long would she be—alone with Reid!—in this God-forsaken cabin? It was too cosy here—well, not cosy, she amended, briefly distracted. There were too many draughts in the rough cabin; the storm was having a field day, exploiting each chink and crack in the thin walls, blowing in under the door.

CHAPTER TEN

NO, COSY wasn't the word, but *intimate* was. If anything, the situation was worse than it had been before their supper. It made her nervous—this whole business of sharing small talk and a meal, of knowing they were stuck here for the night. But it was only one night, she'd been sure; the idea of several days and nights shut in here with Reid—no! It couldn't be!

'But someone must know where we are,' she decided, positive. 'You radioed our position, didn't you?

'I radioed our last known position,' he corrected pleasantly, 'and there may have been a bit of error built into that. Besides, after that we stayed in the air for a fair length of time and travelled some distance.'

'Then why didn't you use the radio again?' she asked, her eyes accusing. 'You could have updated our position.'

'I was busy—remember?—trying to bring us down in one piece. Relax, Kath.' He reached for her hand, grinning when she snatched it away. 'We're in no danger. We've got shelter, plenty of firewood, plenty of food. We could last until spring, if need be.'

'Until *spring*?'

'It won't come to that,' he offered easily. 'We shouldn't be here more than a few days.'

'A few days,' she echoed raggedly. 'We can't—I can't . . . not that long!'

'It's hardly the end of the world,' he pointed out, the soul of reason, then paused to study her through narrowed eyes. 'Unless you can't bear the idea of a few days alone with me.'

'I'd rather not—you must know that.'

'No one better, but I'd thought——' he hesitated briefly, still watching her '—under the circumstances——'

'The circumstances don't make any difference.'

'But consider the alternative,' he advised, getting to his feet, moving into the greater darkness at the far side of the room. 'Surely a few days alone with me are better than being dead.'

'Only barely,' she allowed through gritted teeth, and even in the shadows she caught the quick glint of his smile.

'That's more like it—more like you,' he observed approvingly. 'You made me a little nervous a while ago, with that business of how I'd saved your life. Gratitude never was your style, except at the very start, and I'd hate to think that this adventure had upset the delicate balance we've made of our relationship.'

'So would I,' she agreed with heartfelt sincerity, thankful that he couldn't guess just how delicate her balance had been. It was better now, she noted gratefully. While she couldn't say that Reid's hard edge was back, at least it was threatening to return; she could hear the first signs of it, just beneath his words. Nothing basic had changed, she reminded herself. They still were enemies, bound together only by their grievances—his imagined, hers very real... And don't forget that, not even for a minute! she lectured to herself, watching as Reid emerged from the shadows, bearing a load of blankets.

'What are you doing?'

'Setting us up a place to sleep,' he explained with brief economy, dropping the blankets by the stove, disappearing into the shadows again.

'What's wrong with the bunks?'

'They're too far from the fire. As you pointed out, beggars can't be choosers, but this is clearly a summer place. It isn't insulated...' He broke off to wrestle two of the narrow bunk mattresses into the circle of light by the stove, carefully aligned them, side by side. 'Isn't even caulked,' he resumed, back to the shadows again. 'There's too much cold air coming in, so we'll sleep by the fire.'

'You may...' she informed him, warily eying those two mattresses, side by side, together too narrow to make up the width of a normal double bed. If he seriously thought the two of them were going to sleep like that—*that* close together—he was mad! 'But I'll use one of the bunks. I'll be warm enough.'

'Easy to say now...' he stepped back into the circle of light '...but you'll be singing a different tune long before morning. The stove's not really keeping up with the hellish cold outside.'

'I am not going to sleep on the floor,' she informed him, getting up from the table, moving past him into the shadows to stake a claim on one of the bunks which still had a mattress. 'I'll be fine right here.'

'Suit yourself.' He shrugged, making a point of stacking one of his mattresses on top of the other before he set to work to build up the fire. 'You know,' he continued after a moment, selecting from the wood he'd brought in from the storm, 'for someone who was raised in the tropics, you've got a cavalier attitude about the cold.'

'I've been living in New England for eight years,' she reminded him, beginning to create her own snug nest of blankets. 'I've got used to it.'

'Perhaps it appealed to you,' he observed thoughtfully, laying the logs out to dry beside the stove. 'A cold and proper world, where there isn't room for spontaneity, where you never have to risk taking a chance.'

She stiffened, instantly offended. 'Just because I haven't been willing to go to bed with you——'

'To the point that you'd rather freeze to death than share the fire with me,' he pointed out, grinning. 'Yes, that's one part of it. Dear Malcolm's another.'

'I don't need to listen to this,' she flared. 'I'm going to use the privy, and then go to bed.'

'Want the flashlight?'

'No!' She wanted nothing from Reid—not his help, and certainly not his opinions!—and her righteous anger burned like a flame... until the frigid pitch-dark of the privy snubbed it out. It was incredibly cold in the small space, and she hurried, tripping over her hem again in her haste to get back to the warmth and light of the room.

'Finished?' Reid asked politely, and when she nodded he picked up the flashlight and made his own quick trip. 'Lord, cold enough in there, isn't it?' he asked as he emerged.

She nodded—not that it was all that much warmer in her bunk, she was forced to admit, and it seemed even colder when Reid extinguished the lamp. The darkness was total now, except for one glint of light on the other side of the room, a small triangle of yellowish red which marked the adjustable vent on the door of the wood stove. In the darkness, she shivered, listening to the fierce howl of the wind, the slight sounds Reid made as he crawled into his bed.

He was probably warm as toast, she brooded, staring wide-eyed into the blackness. It was far colder at this end of the room; this corner must leak like a sieve, she fumed—knot-holes like miniature wind tunnels.

She burrowed more deeply into the blankets, drawing them over her face. There, that was better, she assured herself in an attempt at a bracing pep talk. Already her breath was heating the air inside her little cocoon; some warmth! she exulted. Better—far better—to concentrate on that small progress, and ignore just how cold her feet were...

She must have slept for a while; she came awake to realise that the wind had dropped—the high shrieking wail had become a lower, dismal moan. And she was colder, she noted, beginning to shiver. She was cold all over, and her feet were like ice—so cold now that they ached.

Probably frostbite, she concluded gloomily. She'd been so determined to keep her distance from Reid that she was now courting frostbite. There's pride for you! she scolded herself, knowing she had to do something soon.

She'd go to sit by the stove, she decided, carefully levering herself up and out of the bunk. Wrapping a blanket around her like a cloak, she crept towards the warmth, hoping that Reid wouldn't wake, that she could...

'Damn!' She stubbed her toe on something rough, then stumbled, her shoulder connecting with an unknown hard edge. 'Ouch!'

'What the hell...?' Reid's voice, she registered, and nearby in the blackness were the sounds as he stirred. 'Kathy?' he asked, striking a match. 'What are you doing?'

'Try—trying to get to the stove,' she told him through chattering teeth. 'A-and I tripped.'

'Then what...?' The match died; he swore with soft fluency, then struck another and found the kerosene lamp. She closed her eyes against the quick swell of yellow light, kept them closed until she felt Reid draw her close, into the warmth of his embrace. 'You're freezing,' he told her, two words with the sound of accusation in them, then touched her cheek. 'Like ice.'

'I know.'

'Idiot! Don't you have enough sense...?' Abruptly, he deposited her on the bed he'd made for himself. 'I'll build up the fire.'

Numbly, she watched him work, piling plenty of wood on the fire, closing the door with a snap. 'That ought to be better. Do you want me to heat some coffee, or soup?'

'N-no,' she managed, her next words a plaintive wail. 'I just want to be warm.'

'Idiot,' he said again, glaring at her—furious with her, she recognised, cringing, 'but you had to prove your point—anything to stay out of my bed, when it might have occurred to you that, under the circumstances, seduction——' he fairly spat the word at her '—wasn't uppermost in my mind.'

'I'm s-sorry.'

'You should be.' He sighed, running one hand through his hair. 'It's been a long day, Kath, and not the easiest one in the world.'

'I know,' she agreed miserably, caught by a fresh bout of shivering. 'I didn't mean——'

'Of course you did, but you should have known better.' Still angry, he stood for another long moment. Finally he shrugged, surprising her when he sat down beside her, surprising her even more when he reached for her feet. 'Believe it or not, I'm not Superman,' he resumed, absently rubbing circulation back into one icy foot. 'After the work-out we had this afternoon, I wasn't in the mood for sexual acrobatics. I wanted to sleep; I assumed you did too, and I thought we'd be warmer if we slept together.'

'You were right,' she allowed, contrite, but without her previous excess of emotion. And without quite such an excess of shivering, she noted with detachment. She was definitely feeling warmer; the foot he'd been working on no longer ached quite so much. 'I was being silly, I know, but it seemed important to—to...'

'Take a stand, make your point,' he supplied for her, switching his attentions to her other foot, disarming her with his sudden solicitude, by the way his hands were transferring their warmth to her feet, by the intimacy of the moment. 'You do too much of that,' he continued evenly. 'Trying to keep all the emotion out, attaching yourself to someone as cold as Malcolm—— '

'Not Malcolm,' she told Reid, unable to muster the white-hot anger which usually fuelled her exchanges with him. 'Leave him out of this.'

'I'd like to,' he bit out, then softened. 'And you're too tired to fight. Feeling better?' When she nodded, he smiled briefly, relinquishing his hold on her foot. 'Why don't you sleep now, and not back in your frozen bunk. Finish the night here, by the stove.'

'All right.' Obediently, she lay down, holding her breath while he carefully tucked the blankets around her then turned away, clearly preparing to leave her alone. 'What about you?' she dared to ask.

'Good question,' he acknowledged with a brief, twisted smile. 'I'm going to add more wood to the fire, and then I'll——'

'You could come back here,' she suggested shyly. 'You shouldn't have to freeze, just because I've been silly.'

'If you're sure?'

Unexpectedly, she really was, and even more sure when he joined her, drew her to him—into the heat of his body—in a gentle, curiously protective embrace. I can trust him, she thought, already sleepy; for the first time in eight years, I really think I can...

Except for the occasional snap of a burning log in the stove, there was silence when Kathy next awoke. Vaguely, she recognised that the storm was over, and knew, with every fibre of her being, a great sense of contentment. She still lay in Reid's easy embrace, her head cradled on his arm, his hand resting lightly on the curve of her back, his breath gently stirring her hair. He was, she could tell, still sleeping, his breath very even, his body a relaxed, casual sprawl next to hers.

There was no hard edge to him now, she mused, no anger, no challenge. For the time being—a time she wanted to savour—the physical closeness between them was enough . . . like the first days and nights. She wanted to hold on to memory's feeling, to drift—not yet even half awake—beside Reid's sleeping form. But not for long, she realised, sensing the slight change in his breathing before he spoke.

'You're awake,' he observed, his voice without the blurring of first waking—another part of the memory of their time on the boat, when Reid had always been able to be instantly wide awake. 'Feeling better now? Warmer?'

'Mmm,' she allowed lazily, wanting to hold back full consciousness, to remain in this vague and shadowy dream world. She stretched—slow and sensuous, like a cat—her body soft and compliant against the hard line of his. Something else to remember, she realised, caught up in the memories and the moment, caught too by the subtle tension—the desire—building within her, drawing her to him.

She stirred again, or he did; perhaps they both did—not that it mattered, she thought on a quick, in-drawn breath. This was magic, always had been magic, and now she moved instinctively, without conscious thought, her body intensely alive, welcoming his touch, seeking his hidden heat, wanting the magic...

'Tease,' he murmured, laughing.

She froze. What am I doing? she asked herself, the words echoing in the lonely corners of her mind; what have I done? Madness! she knew, the fatal trap. Reid's power over her would be complete, and she could not let that happen. Now, before it was too late, she fought her body's betraying response, willed herself into rigid denial.

'No, don't stop. It's already too late,' he chided, and now his words *were* slightly blurred—not by sleep, but by desire. He moved closer, his lips finding hers, his hands parting the ridiculous bathrobe she wore, capturing her with the clever friction of his touch on her heated skin.

'You'd like to forget this exists, wouldn't you?' he teased, his lips just touching hers in a feather-light kiss. 'You'd like to be as cold as dear Malcolm——'

'No, don't,' she managed against the claims of his touch. 'Leave him out of this.'

'He will be, sweet, before we're done,' Reid promised, his laughter in the darkness before his mouth closed over hers. It was deliberate, the way he branded her, kissed her with a deep, probing expertise beyond her power to resist, kissed all her defences away, melting the ice she hadn't known was around her heart—eight years of ice, she thought with a pang.

She was lost and didn't care, not when he made this kind of magic for her. She had no choice but to reach out to him, her body instinctively arching into his, aching to remove the final distance he still maintained between them. Lost, she thought again, her hands tempting him to feel what she felt, and knew she'd succeeded when she heard his voice, the words like an incantation...

'That's right,' he was saying. 'That's right... Ah, yes, Kath,' he breathed—was he as lost as she was? she wondered, the idea intensely exciting, driving her to greater daring. 'Ah...yes,' he said again and, finally unable to maintain his control, drew her closer, then closer still. 'So good, Kath... Lord, you haven't changed!'

Nothing had, she learned from their wild and instinctive journey of discovery. They still knew how to please each other, how to caress and kiss, how to drive each other to the edge. There in the quiet darkness—no need for light, not when they remembered so well—they explored the limits of sensation, fully shared—even revelled in—the intensity of their feeling.

Love? she wondered, and knew it couldn't be—not after all the anger, the pain of his betrayal—yet it felt like love. The care they took, the pleasure in giving and receiving—it felt like love, and something deeper, something more elemental...

She wanted him, needed his fire to fill the endless, aching void within her, needed the completion only he could give. And he did give; she *knew* how totally, how carefully he gave himself to her, led her to the final sharp intensity, the all-consuming blaze of their union.

Finally, when their storm had ended, he held her close and spoke into the darkness. 'It's always been that way for us,' he told her. 'The one thing we can't deny.'

Nor would she try. Eight long, lonely years left her starved, but still... The truth had been too obvious; he too could feel it, admit it. In this, at least, they were equals—equals in what they must acknowledge, in what they had lost.

'Most couples, I think, would say this is enough,' Reid mused, his voice curiously flat, the emptiness emphasised when he released her and turned on to his back, close to her but no longer touching. 'They'd say that the physical part is enough of a reason to maintain the marriage.'

'For you, perhaps,' she countered, discovering that the concealing cloak of darkness gave her courage. It was easier to be honest when she couldn't see Reid, when he couldn't see her. 'Not for me.'

'I know. You've made that abundantly clear.'

But only when... not until...

'You wanted something else, didn't you?' he continued, depriving her of any chance to defend herself. 'Funny, for most girls, if not love then it's money that drives them, but money never seemed to matter to you.'

'It didn't,' she supplied, but she doubted he heard. He wasn't conducting a conversation so much as thinking aloud. She could see him in her mind's eye, lying beside her but at a distance—a very real distance now. She imagined his arms were crossed behind his head, his eyes were open to stare into the darkness.

'I was never sure what did matter to you,' he resumed after a moment. 'A way off the island—that's what you said at the start, but I was never quite sure... I thought—and this may amuse you—that perhaps you had a kind of schoolgirl crush, that you believed it was love at first sight...

'But you weren't what I thought,' he resumed after a moment. 'I'd misread you, thought you were one of life's innocents——'

'Do we have to go through this?' she broke in, acutely uncomfortable. She had enough; she didn't like hearing herself dissected like this. 'There's no point——'

'But there is,' he contradicted sharply—finally some emotion, if only anger, back in his voice. 'I'm trying to get you out of my system.'

'I hoped you'd just done that.'

'What—the sex?' he asked, deliberately cruel. 'I'll never get that part of you out of my system. We're too compatible, Kath, but what I can't understand...' he turned back to her, rising up on one arm, she guessed, as though—in spite of the darkness—he was looking down, searching her face for clues to his puzzle '...is how someone so cold, so deliberate, can be so responsive. Fire and ice...such a paradox there,' he brooded, his intensity palpable in the charged space between them. 'Fire and ice,' he said again, catching a few strands of her hair, sifting them through his fingers. 'What is it about you, I wonder? What made you that way?'

You did! she thought, biting her lip to hold back the words. The fire came from loving you, from wanting you to love me, to be there for me...and the ice is simple—the only protection I had after you...

'What drives you?' he persisted, interrupting the thought she knew was best left hidden away. 'Not money—if you'd just wanted money, you wouldn't have left . . . I brought you to New York, which was what you wanted.'

'No! It wasn't New York; it was never New York! All I wanted was just to get away from the island, to get out of Paulette's life and Thom's. Anyway, that was just at the start, and then . . .' She caught herself.

'Yes?' he enquired with a kind of silky menace. 'And then what?'

Then I was so much in love with you—another thought to censor. 'Then things—things got complicated,' she amended weakly. 'You left me alone——'

'Not that you seemed to suffer,' he put in unpleasantly. 'You certainly found ways to keep busy.'

'Busy?' she asked with a bitter smile, remembering all those lonely times. 'Just what do you think I was doing?'

'Heaven knows. Having an affair—given how much you enjoyed that kind of activity. For a while, dear wife, I wondered about you and Greg.'

'Greg?' she echoed, indignant and incredulous in equal parts. 'Gregory? How could you think that?'

'Don't worry, sweet, I didn't—not for long. Greg's too loyal to me, and he'd never have satisfied someone with your——' he paused, then resumed with bitter humour '—your special gifts.

'A funny thing, though,' he continued, impersonal again, a stranger in the darkness. 'Greg's a lot like dear Malcolm—conservative, inhibited . . . You do latch on to the strangest men.'

'I don't latch on——'

'Of course you do. I was the first—obviously a mistake, although I did do what you expected of me. I took you away from the island, and then—an unexpected bonus—I got you to the States, gave you time to get your bearings and decide what would come next. Not a bad bargain there—the sex was good, and I think——'

'I don't give a damn what you think,' Kathy exploded, white-hot anger finally driving her past the limit of prudence, 'and I am not going to lie here and let you play games with my head!'

'I don't see why not. You were willing enough to lie here and let me play other games.'

'That was a mistake. I was still half asleep, and——'

'Spare me,' he broke in, all worldly sophistication and ironic amusement. 'Don't try to tell me that you didn't know what you were doing.'

'I'm not going to...' She stopped, putting more distance between them, grabbing a blanket to wrap tightly around her. When she opened her eyes, she saw that the night was over—thank heaven for that! she thought when she saw the light working into the cabin through knotholes, through small breaks in the walls, through the cracks in the boards which covered the windows. There was light enough now for her to distinguish shapes and shadows: the wood Reid had left to dry on the floor, their clothes spread out on chairs drawn close to the stove. 'I won't discuss it,' she told him—a childish defence, but the only one she could manage at the moment.

Mercifully, he accepted her decision—perhaps he too had tired of the game he'd been playing. Protected now by a blend of armed truce and intense loathing, they worked together to produce a scratch breakfast. Having a task steadied her; by the time they sat down at the table she had lost most of her defensive self-consciousness, was able to make a reasonable meal of the canned ham and beans they'd heated on the stove. Afterwards, while she finished the last of her coffee, Reid left the table to prowl the small confines of the cabin—like a caged lion, she thought, warily watching him, relieved when he finally reached for his jacket.

'I'm going out to take a look around,' he announced as he made for the door.

'Fine,' she snapped, getting up as the door slammed behind them. Automatically, she began to clear away the remains of their breakfast, determined to keep busy, determined not to think about what had happened between them.

Reid was gone for a long time; in fact, for more than two hours she had been resolutely refusing to wonder what was keeping him so long. In that time, she had thoroughly tidied the cabin and had a pot of canned stew warming on the wood stove. Lacking anything to read in the cabin, she was dusting when the door opened, permitting a cold draught to spill into the room.

'How remarkably domestic,' Reid observed drily, and Kathy turned, dust cloth in hand, to find him framed in the open doorway, a large and forbidding shadow, back-lit by the clear white light reflecting off the snow. 'A pot simmering on the stove and my wife hard at work, dusting... Sweetheart, this isn't like you.'

'How would you know?'

'Past experience,' he told her, pausing on the doorstep to stamp the snow from his boots. 'Remember? We did live together for a few weeks, and I don't recall——' he interrupted himself to move into the room, took the chair closest to the stove and pulled off his boots '—that you ever did anything that could remotely be called housework—no cooking, no cleaning.'

'Don't tell me you've held that against me for all these years!'

'I've had more than that to hold against you,' he corrected, stretching his long legs out towards the warmth of the stove. 'It puzzled me—like so much else about you. You seemed such a sweet, simple girl, and I'd assumed you'd enjoy that kind of thing—fussing about, playing happy homemaker.'

She bit her lip, those days vivid again in her mind. 'You think I had any choice in the matter?'

He shrugged. 'You could have done whatever you pleased. I wouldn't have denied you.'

'*You* didn't have to,' she observed bitterly. 'You had a cook who didn't want any help in the kitchen, and a cleaning service coming in every day——'

'Which must have pleased you no end,' he put in smoothly. 'Greg said you were almost never at home, that you were usually out in pursuit of culture and social polish.'

'What else could I do?' she cried out, the present receding, all the old grievances fresh again in her mind. 'You weren't there, I had no friends, and your mother certainly wasn't going to take me in hand! And besides, culture was Gregory's idea, and—— '

'A convenient excuse—it was all someone else's fault, was it?' Reid enquired, eyeing her coldly.

'I never said that, but I'd expected that we'd be together.'

'What? A blissful twosome, living alone in a romantic vacuum for the rest of our lives?'

'Of course not.'

'Then what?'

'I didn't know! How could I?' She gestured in mute appeal, the dust cloth still clutched in one hand. 'I had no idea how you lived, what you did for a living, what it was like to live in New York.'

'Yet you wanted New York——'

'No!' She nearly stamped her foot in frustration, wondering why—even now—it was so important to make herself understood. 'I wanted out of the islands, just to go somewhere—anywhere—in the States, where I could make something of myself.'

'Exactly.' He stared at her long and hard, assessing, judging her, coming to some conclusions. 'You wanted to do your own thing, wanted to *be* yourself, *by* yourself. It must have been all those years knocking around the islands, drifting from one place to another . . . no ties, no relationships to hold you back.'

She shook her head, not liking the image he was constructing. 'There was my father, and then Paulette——'

'Who was hardly a paragon of concerned interest. She knew nothing about me, had met me less than twenty-four hours before, and yet she was perfectly willing to let you go off with me.'

'Paulette owed me nothing! She had already done more for me than I had any right to expect. She wasn't responsible for me.'

'Yes . . .' From his place by the stove, Reid cast her a brief, appraising glance. 'It seems that no one has ever felt responsible for you.'

'That isn't true! There was my father——'

'Whose idea of responsibility was to drag you from island to island, with no permanent home, nothing settled, no real direction.'

'That suited me fine!'

'Precisely.' Reid smiled, coolly triumphant. 'You've just proved my point. You're a loner, Kath. You don't want anyone, won't let anyone in. All you wanted from me was a base and the means to start your new life. Once I'd given you that, you cut me out.'

Oh, that was rich! she told herself, worrying the frayed ends of the dust cloth. There he sat, the world's expert at cutting people out—at cutting her out, anyway—accusing *her* of not letting anyone in when it was all *his* fault! Once they'd been married, he'd turned so cold . . . He'd shut her out of his life—all but *abandoned* her, for heaven's sake!—and now he was trying to blame the whole thing on her. 'Fine,' she finally managed, her tone not quite as even as she would have liked. 'If it pleases you to believe that——'

'If it pleases me?' he cut in, repeating her words with harsh mockery. 'Can you give me one good reason why

I shouldn't believe—shouldn't *know*—that you'd never had any intention of making our marriage work?'

'If it ever *was* a real marriage,' she shot back quickly, her only defence—and a poor one, at that—against the feelings rising within her. Lord, he had broken her heart, she remembered. His cavalier disregard for their marriage—for her—had nearly destroyed her, and now... 'And even if it was legal, you hardly gave either one of us a chance to make it work. You went away——'

'I was working,' he snapped, clearly impatient with her. 'That's where I had to be, at that point—building experience in the field, learning what I'd need to know when I could finally begin to take over from my father. Sure, it was a family business, but that didn't mean I could just coast. I was expected to do my share, and I damn well wanted everyone to know that I was something more than the boss's son. I had to work, Kath! I couldn't spend my whole life with you.'

'Could spend almost none of it with me, in fact, and couldn't even bother to explain it to me.' She glared at him, across a distance of misunderstanding, not space. 'You brought me to New York, and then dumped me! If it hadn't been for Gregory and Aunt Margaret, I'd...' Her voice wavered, then broke; regardless, she stumbled on. 'I'd have had no one... nothing at all.'

'Oh, well done, Kath,' he mocked, on his feet now, stalking her. 'But I'm not convinced. You wanted no one...' He stopped just before her, crowding her back against one of the bunks. 'Wanted nothing from me.'

'That's not true,' she protested, forced to look up to meet his blazing gaze. 'I did want...' She paused to edit herself—determined to keep away from the humiliation which waited at the core of the truth. 'At least, just at first I did want to be with you, and I never wanted to be alone. But you left me, with nothing but Gregory as a go-between, and I hated it! I wanted *something*, something of my own.'

'Yes, sooner or later it had to come down to this.' He caught her unawares, captured her by the shoulders, gripping her with painful force. 'I was never sure what game you were playing,' he told her, 'but I *knew* it would come down to this—poor little Kathy, all alone in the world, and wanting something... A baby? Are you trying to tell me that a baby would have solved all your problems?'

Here it was, she realised, closing her eyes against him, against the pain still as fresh and as new as it had ever been. Here it was, that final barrier—impossibly hurtful and cruel, the one thing they had never discussed face to face... Only through Gregory, she thought, wishing with all her heart that it could have remained that way. 'I...' She shook her head, fighting the swift constriction in her throat. 'Please... don't ask me that.'

'Why not? Does the truth hurt now?' he asked with terrible menace. 'Or is it just that you'd rather I didn't know? It's understandable, I'll grant you that—the truth hardly matches the image you've tried to create—but it won't work.

'All those years, Kath,' he mused, his tone lighter now—lighter, yes, but cloaked in a hard, bitter anger. 'All those years when you thought that I didn't know, when you must have believed that you'd kept your secret from me... and you would have, if only you hadn't told Gregory.'

Finally, Kathy opened her eyes. If she hadn't told Gregory what? her thoughts screamed, her mind caught in a strange, off-balance confusion which finally compelled her to look up at Reid. 'What are you talking about?'

'You know damn well what I'm talking about,' he bit out. 'There's no point in pretending, because Gregory told me—something you should have expected. No matter how hard you tried to dazzle him, he worked for me; the firm provided his paycheque. We'd bought his loyalty, my father and I; you never stood a chance.'

'A chance at what?' she cried, completely bewildered. 'I don't know what——'

'Damn you, give it up!' Reid glared down at her, his grip on her shoulders suddenly stronger, biting into her flesh. 'I don't know what your game is—perhaps you've been trying to fool yourself, wanting to think that you were the one wronged—but it won't work. I won't *let* it work, because I know your dirty little secret! I've known from the start.'

'Known what?'

'About the baby—our child,' he stressed with undisguised venom. 'The one you—do you want me to say that ugly word, Kath?' he demanded, shaking her slightly, his rage barely contained. 'I'm talking about your abortion, about the baby you refused to carry to term.'

CHAPTER ELEVEN

'THE baby...' she managed before she had to stop, despair a scalding heat, a freezing cold, a pain past bearing, an absolute agony. 'I don't...' She could get no further, couldn't say the word, but... 'Refused?' she echoed hollowly, focusing on that one false note. 'Refused?' she said again, because there was a reality here, one which didn't belong, had nothing to do with the pain. 'That isn't right... I didn't——'

'Spare me,' Reid said savagely. 'Give it up!'

Spare *him*? she thought, her pain instantly transformed to blinding rage. 'I never *refused*! Don't accuse me of doing what you would have told me to do, if you'd known in time.'

'If I'd known what?' he asked, but she was past attending to his words.

'I was just a toy to you,' she hurried on, the storm of bitter memory unleased. 'You didn't want to be saddled with a wife and a child... "Perhaps it's for the best", you said. You——'

'That's not right!' He frowned, eyes narrowed to study her face. 'I never told you that; I never saw you after that! You'd left before I knew.'

'Spare *me*,' she all but shrieked. 'You knew! You knew—Gregory told you!'

'That's right,' he agreed, the two words clipped and cold. 'All I *ever* knew I learned from Gregory. *You*...' Reid stopped abruptly, drew one harsh breath, mastering the worst of his anger before continuing. 'You couldn't be bothered to tell me anything—not that you were pregnant, not that you'd decided that you didn't want a child, not that you'd got rid of it, not——'

'I didn't do that! I——' Her turn, now, to pause. How could he have made himself believe such a lie? she wondered bitterly, but she already knew, and the hurt was that much the worse for the knowing. His guilt had forced him to believe she was guilty of his secret wish. He'd made her the villain, damn him, she cursed, fighting for control, fighting the sudden mist of tears. 'You can't keep lying to yourself, blaming me...'

'I know the truth.'

'You don't! I lost...' She wrenched herself free of his bruising grip on her shoulders, turned away from his blazing gaze. 'I lost the baby,' she started again, her voice flat and lifeless, no more than a whisper as those days of desolation engulfed her. Now—finally, after so many years—she was remembering everything, finally saying all she'd held within her for so long... so very long. 'I lost the baby. It just happened, without a reason... and the doctor said it was just one of those things—that we could try again... and I wondered—how are we going to try again when you're so far away, when that's where you want to be, and you won't even answer my letters——?'

'That's not true,' Reid broke in harshly. 'None of it!'

'But it is. Do you think I'd make it up?' she asked through her tears, forcing herself to turn back to him, read his flat rejection of her and the truth in his eyes. Damn you! she thought with a wild flare of defiance, the compelling need to shake his eight years of smug complacency. 'Damn you, it's time that you faced the truth—and I can *prove* it! You can see my doctor—a perfectly respectable obstetrician, not some dirty back-alley quack in league with me to abort my baby and then pretend it happened naturally! I'll give you his name and address—he's in New York, Park Avenue, all very proper and upstanding,' she continued recklessly, ignoring the sudden new shading of doubt in Reid's eyes, the sudden pain. 'Talk to him! Ask him why I lost the baby *you* said was better left unborn!'

'No,' Reid breathed, his face set in rigid lines, drained of all colour. 'Kath, is this true?'

'Every word,' she spat out. 'You *know* it is!'

'No! No—I only knew what Gregory told me, what Gregory...' He stopped, and an instant of cool calculation clouded his gaze before he continued. 'Gregory—he was our only link, wasn't he? You never called——'

'But I wrote,' Kathy countered, defending herself. 'He said I couldn't get through by phone, so I wrote. I wrote stacks of letters! I wrote one every day——'

'And gave them to him to deliver to me?'

'You know I did.'

'Do I?'

'*Yes*,' she insisted, furious with him for making her restate the obvious, the already known. What was it? Had Reid spent all these years pretending that she was the one who had stopped the communication between them? Surely he knew better than to try that kind of pretence, and yet... There was something going on here, she suddenly realised, something about Reid's expression... It had been years since she'd seen it, but she hadn't forgotten that look. Eyes narrowed, he was staring at some unknown point in the distance, and she knew that behind his careful, expressionless mask his mind would be working at a quick pace, weighing the facts, using logic to connect with some truth beyond her discernment. 'What is it?' she asked.

'Gregory.'

That one word hung in the air between them, echoing, reverberating, forcing her to rethink, to sort through all the implications. Gregory? What had Gregory to do with the two of them, and why this sudden change in Reid's whole attitude? His anger towards her was suddenly gone, replaced by something different—an indefinable sense that he no longer blamed her. 'What about Gregory?'

'Don't you see?' Reid prompted. 'Gregory was our go-between, the one link between us, but he gave me no letters. I never had *any* letters from you.'

'That's impossible! I——'

'None,' he continued, ignoring—perhaps not even hearing—her interruption. 'At the start, he explained that you'd said that you weren't much for writing letters. Then towards the end he said you were having too good a time, that you were much too busy to write.'

Too busy? What a laugh that was, she thought with a brief, twisted smile. 'That's a lie!'

'One of several, it would appear. Kathy...' He paused, taking her hands, something protective in his light touch, something gentle—something oddly at variance with the hard, cold glint she could see in his eyes. 'Greg told *you* that I didn't want to have a child yet, then told *me* that you'd had an abortion.'

'That's your story,' she countered hotly. 'Your lie.'

'No, it's the truth.' He hesitated for an instant, then tried again. 'Look, if I'm prepared to believe you, can't you believe me?'

'I doubt it.' She snatched her hands from his grasp, crossed her arms tightly—a defence, an attempt to contain the excess of emotion which threatened to overwhelm her. Trust Reid? How could she, when she'd lived for eight years with his betrayal? Trust him now, just because he was no longer angry with her, because he seemed to be trying for reason and understanding between them? 'I—why would Gregory lie?'

'You tell me,' Reid returned coolly. 'You were with him far more than I was. Perhaps he wanted you for himself.'

'*Gregory*?' she burst out, incredulous. 'He's not like that; *I'm* not like that! There was nothing——'

'Are you sure?'

'Of course I'm sure! What are you thinking—that we had an affair?'

'That Greg might have wanted one with you.'

'If he did, he kept it a secret,' Kathy flared. 'He was just there, looking after me—no more than what you'd told him to do. I never had any sense that he cared about me... He was your employee, and I never forgot that his first loyalty was to you—and after I left New York I never heard from him again.'

'No contact at all?' Reid asked, saw her quick nod and was off again, his mind employing clear logic, testing known facts against an obscured reality. 'Then what about support cheques?'

'What about them?' She gave him a scornful look. 'I wanted nothing from you, wouldn't have taken——'

'I've been paying you since the start,' Reid cut in. 'Every month, just like clockwork, I sign the cheque, Greg mails it off, and you cash it... or is that a lie, too?' he asked, reading her expression. '*Have* you taken any money from me? No, of course not,' he answered for her, briefly closing his eyes. 'Something else for Greg to explain... and I trusted him!'

'Your right-hand man, your *alter ego*,' Kathy offered with a bitter but tremulous edge. 'I used to wonder if you really believed that having Gregory look after me was enough to keep me happy—that I wouldn't care if you weren't around, so long as there was someone to take care of...' Her voice wavered, then broke. Her pride in tatters, she had to force herself to continue to meet Reid's gaze, permit him to see how much it had hurt—how much it *still* hurt... how much she had cared, and still did. 'It wasn't,' she began again, summoning up the last of her reserves, 'what I'd expected.'

'No.' The word hung between them for a moment, until—and with a muffled oath—Reid drew her close. 'Oh, Kath,' he breathed, and then—incredibly, it seemed, his thoughts had run in parallel with hers, 'It hurt so much . . . to be without you, to come home and find you gone . . .' He drew her even closer—insistently, compulsively—against the hard, taut line of him, holding her as though he'd never let her go.

'It was hell,' he told her, his voice uneven, all emotion—from the heart, she knew. 'And then, when he told me what had happened to the baby, that hurt even more—I couldn't forgive you for that final betrayal . . .'

'I know,' she whispered though tears she hadn't known were there—remembering, feeling all his pain because it would have been so like her own. 'I know,' she said again, crying harder now, reliving all the pain, the loneliness. 'It was so hard . . .'

'And I wasn't there. I would have been, sweet Kath,' he promised her, his own voice still unsteady. 'I would have been . . . Dear lord, I wish I'd known!'

But now he knew; this time he held her close, shared her pain and shared her tears . . . this excess of emotion a healing balm, drawing them together, tearing down the barriers.

'Finally,' he murmured later, when the storm had passed. 'Kath, sweetheart . . . it never stopped. I always loved you, always wanted you.'

'I felt the same way too,' she confessed shyly, linking her arms around his neck, lifting her face to the sudden insistence of his lips. 'It never stopped,' she managed, before his mouth closed over hers, seared her with his need, ignited hers.

This time, she dimly recognised, was unlike any other. The empty years—too many years!—had left them without defences, with no pretence, no calculation. This time his kiss was an endless hunger, her response a desperate need, their world a timeless one of passion and desire.

Later, they would remember only fragments of this new reality: his clever touch and her spontaneous response, her own sudden daring and his ragged declaration of his love and her own breathless answer, the quick, compelling need to banish the last barriers between them, the joyous abandon with which they came together—close, so close, closer than ever before, then closer still... into a final oneness which could not be denied.

'All those wasted years...' Afterwards, when they lay in an easier embrace, finally satisfied, complete, she heard his rueful murmur.

'But no more,' she countered fiercely. 'They're over now.'

'Mmm, but still a waste, sweetheart... although——' he paused long enough to raise himself up on one elbow, smiled down at her '—you're twice the girl you were eight years ago.'

'Why?' she asked, bolder now in spite of the quick flush of colour which stained her cheeks. 'Because I'm better now at this—at making love?'

'That, too,' he acknowledged carelessly, lifting one of her hands, examining its slender strength, 'but you're better now at everything, more capable... I remember that first night, when I walked in and heard you rabbiting on about the church. You were so enchantingly earnest, you knew your stuff... and I fell in love with you all over again.'

'You couldn't have,' she objected lazily. 'You still hated me.'

'True, but while I was still hating you I was falling in love with what you'd become—the woman, not the girl I'd known before.'

'You had a funny way of showing it.'

'I was fighting it—fighting for my life, or so I thought.' He leaned forward, still holding her hand, dropped a kiss on her open palm. 'Weren't you?'

'Yes,' she acknowledged. 'I hated the way you made me feel. I'd worked so hard to be independent, and seeing you made me remember too much. Suddenly, it was eight years ago; I was pathetically young, and you were a man of the world.'

'I never was quite such a man of the world as you may have thought,' he confessed with a self-conscious smile. 'Eight years ago, I was still a boy—a bad case of arrested development, as my father was fond of pointing out. I still thought life was a game, all playtime and fun...

'Which was part of the problem,' he continued after a moment's reflection. 'I'm afraid that—just at first—what I felt for you was infatuation. That first night on the beach, when you stood there, wearing that virginal nightgown and that silk shawl... Well, you were mad to think you could trust me, to think that you could ask me to take you off the island and that nothing would happen. I already wanted to have you, to *possess* you——'

'Which was all I wanted,' Kathy put in quickly. 'To be with you, to be whatever you wanted me to be.'

'Probably not the best basis for a marriage,' Reid allowed, cool logic accompanied by a wry smile. 'All smoke and mirrors and damn little substance.'

'Yes,' Kathy acknowledged uncomfortably, and felt a fresh stirring of doubt. 'So how do we know there's more to it this time?'

'Because you've grown up,' he answered promptly. 'Perhaps we both have—but you, sweetheart, have developed a mind of your own. You exceeded my wildest expectations that day you took after me about damaging your groined arch. Lord, you were enchanting, all hell-fire and brimstone; no way was I going to win that round from you!'

'You were sick, you passed out on me,' she reminded him. 'That's why you lost.'

'I'd have lost anyway,' he countered quickly. 'By that time, we'd already gone enough rounds for me to see that you weren't about to let me possess you—except when it's what you want too.'

'Which seems to be most of the time——'

'And proves my point,' he finished, pleased, dropping a kiss on her forehead. 'We're right for each other now, Kath, and I love you more than I did at the start. I love your fire——' he paused, kissed one eyelid closed, then the other '—your strength and your passion.' He paused again, his lips poised just above hers. 'I love all that you are, all that you've become,' he told her, his voice deepening, less even now, coloured by the fresh stirring of his desire, her answering need. 'I love the woman those wasted years made of the girl, and I'm going to have her... if she'll have me?'

'I don't have much choice,' she acknowledged honestly, returning his brief, teasing kiss. 'I never stopped loving you, even when I was afraid to admit it.'

'Then it's settled... No more bad times, sweetheart,' he promised. 'We're together, and no one can tear us apart. And with luck,' he continued, drawing her closer, the gleam in his eye leaving no doubt as to his intentions, 'it will be spring before anyone finds us...'

'*Why*, damn you? Why did you do it?' Reid asked, speaking very quietly, but with a blazing intensity. 'What did you hope to accomplish?'

Predictably, Gregory blustered, presenting a picture of innocent confusion—after all, Kathy reminded herself, he'd got away with it for eight years, probably would never have been exposed if the plane hadn't gone down, if she and Reid hadn't had three days alone in the cabin.

Their rescue—although, in Kathy's opinion, 'rescue' was too dramatic a word—had been quick and easy. A search plane had spotted them in the morning; the rescue team, snowmobiles snarling, had arrived a few hours later. There had been a bit of a scramble to get the two of them back down the mountain before the light faded—

as simple as that, Kathy had marvelled as they had arrived at the nearby fire station which had served as command post for the effort.

There had been media there—a few reporters and a TV camera crew. Reid had answered some questions while Kathy had stood beside him, blinded by the harsh lights which turned night into brighter than day. For a few minutes, there had been a general air of celebration; she and Reid had been surrounded by those who had searched for them while others, hearing the news, had begun arriving to see for themselves that the search had successfully ended.

Gregory had been one of the latecomers, his fine wool overcoat and dark suit incongruous in the crowd of ski parkas and rough hunting jackets. Kathy had seen him almost immediately—all cool and smooth poise, except for his eyes, which were shaded with doubt and anxiety... As well they should be! she'd thought, shocked by the depth and strength of her anger.

Perhaps some of that anger had transmitted itself to Reid; he'd had his arm around her and might have sensed the sudden tension within her. He'd been talking to someone, had paused to cast her a brief, puzzled glance, before making a quick survey of the room. '*So*! Time for unfinished business,' he'd murmured to her, then—offering an excuse to those around them—he'd propelled them both through the crowd. 'Greg, in there,' he ordered with a brief nod towards the empty office just beyond where they were standing.

Now the three of them were alone, closeted in this small room. His arm still around her, drawing her close, Reid confronted Gregory—who would have looked innocent, Kathy acknowledged, had it not been for his eyes. They were too busy, searching wildly for a safe haven, unwilling to focus on either Kathy or Reid. 'Why did I do what?' he asked now, palms open in a gesture of complete ignorance. 'I'm not sure what you're talking about.'

'You know damn well what I'm talking about!' Reid swore briefly under his breath. 'You *lied*—to Kath and to me—you broke up our marriage, for heaven's sake!'

'Lied about what?'

'About our child,' Reid bit out, anger and pain both alive in his tone. 'You told me she'd had an abortion, told her that I'd said losing the child was for the best.'

'Is that her story?' Gregory countered with a nice touch of indignation and shocked incredulity. 'I knew it! I knew this would happen—that if the two of you were alone for a few days——'

'We'd learn the truth,' Reid supplied with icy venom.

'No, not that.' Gregory shook his head—very smooth now, Kathy noted, very sure of himself. 'I knew that she'd lie to you, twist things... do whatever she could to make you believe that *she* was the innocent party... pure as the driven snow,' he added with a bitter laugh.

'You really don't know her, Reid,' he continued, all earnest concern now. 'You don't know what she's capable of, but I *do*! I've spent more time with her than you have, and I *know*. I was there when she killed that baby——'

'How *dare* you?' Kathy burst in, her anger white-hot. 'That's a lie!'

'Yes, you would say so, would like to believe it,' Gregory noted with a brief, pitying look in her direction, then turned back to Reid. 'She's lying. She lies all the time. I was there then, and I saw what she was like—what she's *still* like. She hasn't changed, Reid. When you were hospitalised, I saw enough of her to know that she hadn't changed. You can't trust her, can't believe what she says. She twists things——'

'And you think that's what she did while we were together these last few days?'

'I'm sure she did,' Gregory allowed, sounding pained. 'She'll never forgive me for telling you the truth—she made that very clear while you were in the hospital—and I'm guessing that she did her best to paint me as the villain. God knows what kind of lies she came up with... anything—*anything*!—to make you believe her.'

'And—what?' Reid asked, in a tone of polite disinterest, his anger suddenly gone—was Gregory winning? Kathy wondered, feeling cold, a little sick when Reid withdrew his arm from her shoulders. Was Gregory going to ruin things again? Was Reid going to *let* him? 'Don't you think I'm capable of seeing through her lies?'

'No,' Gregory answered frankly. 'You've never been able to be objective about her. You let your emotions get in the way—like the last time, when she got rid of the baby, then walked away... well, you know you took that pretty hard.'

An admission, Kathy realised in the moment of silence which followed Gregory's words. 'Got rid of the baby,' he'd said. 'Walked away'—proof positive that what Reid had told her was true.

Not, of course, that she had doubted him; she hadn't. There was that new, indefinable rapport between them, a current, highly charged, that was trust... at least on her side. But what about Reid? How could she be sure that he trusted her, would continue to trust her, now that Gregory was doing his best to ruin things one last time?

'Reid, I'm only trying to help,' Gregory began again, breaking the silence with his appeal. 'I don't want to see you hurt all over again!'

'Don't worry about me,' Reid advised, a glint of something like amusement in his voice. 'I'm older now, wiser too—I'm not so likely to be taken in by a tangle of lies——' but *whose* lies? Kathy asked herself, frightened, wishing Reid wouldn't sound quite so non-committal, so—so ambiguous! '—as I was eight years ago.'

'But you don't know how she can twist the truth,' Gregory put in quickly. 'Eight years ago, I had to sort out her story, get at the truth. *You* didn't have to deal with her lies!'

'True,' Reid agreed evenly. 'I wasn't given the chance to deal with anything, was I?'

'Which seemed best——'

'From your point of view, I'll just bet it did,' Reid observed, and for the first time Kathy heard a scornful note in his voice—not much, but of some comfort to her. 'That time, everything went your way.'

'What——?'

'And you thought you'd never have to answer for what you'd done,' Reid persisted, overriding the other man's attempt to break in. 'Quite a shock, wasn't it, to learn that Kath and I were working together? You must have hoped that we were still too angry with one another, or that the past was too painful for either of us to bring it up.'

'I...' Gregory shifted uneasily. 'I don't know what you're talking about.'

'You damn well do!' Reid's scorn suddenly shifted, transformed into blazing anger, palpable but still well controlled. 'Did you seriously think Kath and I could spend three days together—three days and three nights all alone—without at least making a start at untangling your skein of lies?'

'I—heaven knows what she said,' Gregory blustered. 'That lying bitch——'

'That's enough!' Reid's patience snapped—if patience were really what it had been. The transformation frightened Gregory; it even frightened Kathy, who had never seen Reid quite so angry. 'Don't you ever—*ever*!—say something like that again. Don't you ever *try* something like that again!'

'I only wanted to explain——'

'No, you only wanted—one last time—to save your neck, but it won't work. You had your chance; I gave you time—I hoped, even after all you'd done, that the years might count for something, that you might admit what we both know is true.' Reid paused, drew one long breath before continuing. 'Now all I want to know is why—why in God's name did you do it?'

'I don't...' Gregory began, then stopped. He, like Kathy, had seen Reid shift his stance, had seen him lean forward, towering over the other man, his hands balled into fists. It was enough for Gregory, and his bravado crumbled. 'For your father,' he admitted miserably. 'He and your mother didn't think that Ka—that is, they felt your marriage had been a mistake.'

'So you took it upon yourself to ruin it?'

'It wasn't *my* idea,' Gregory countered, pleading now. 'Your father said—and he was still my boss then—that I should do what I could, that I should try—that there might be possibilities, with you away and out of touch. He told me that the first thing I should do was make sure that you and Kathy couldn't communicate directly...'

'So you pocketed her letters, lied to me——'

'I *had* to,' Gregory attempted to explain. 'My job was on the line.'

'You should have come to me,' Reid told him savagely. 'I would have handled it.'

'You weren't in control then; your father was,' Gregory reminded him. 'You didn't hire and fire; your father did, and he'd made it clear...I had no choice, and he was getting impatient... He said that anyone who wanted to succeed, who wanted a real place in the company—and with him—had damn well better learn to innovate and improvise. "Seize the moment!" is what he said, and so, when Kathy lost the baby——'

'You saw your chance, and took it,' Reid supplied, his voice like ice. 'Did my father reward you well?'

'I kept my job,' Gregory announced with a self-serving edge. 'I wasn't after money.'

'But you got money, didn't you?' Reid persisted. 'You broke up my marriage—my father would have paid you well for that.'

'But you never got a divorce,' Gregory qualified—didn't he realise, Kathy wondered, that he was only digging himself a deeper hole? 'That was what your father wanted—what your mother wanted most of all. I wasn't as successful as they'd hoped I'd be.'

'So they reduced the reward,' Reid stated flatly, 'and you made it up with all those years of support payments I thought I was making to Kathy.'

'What? The support cheques?' Gregory asked, attempting one last bluff. 'Did she try to tell you that she never got them?'

'And succeeded,' Reid snapped. 'Don't try it. Greg. Be grateful that I'm not going to press criminal charges on that little detail.'

'But——'

'Don't push me too much more! Right now it wouldn't take much—not much at all—to see you hang,' Reid warned, softly ominous—but also, Kathy sensed, tired of this long revelation, as sickened by it as she was. 'You're through, Greg—finished with me, finished with the firm. Effective now, you're fired. You will not be permitted to enter your office; you may not take anything away. If there are personal items, they'll be sent to you. That's it. Leave now.' He moved then to open the office door—flung it back, actually, so that it crashed against the cinder-block wall, the sound reverberating in the sudden silence created by that one violent gesture. Then, the anger now apparently out of his system, he waited—a tall, remote figure, watching impassively as Gregory brushed past him.

'Just a detail I needed to handle,' Reid apologised to the rescue workers grouped in a circle just outside the door, all of them wearing expressions of intense curiosity, avid to know why the sudden outburst and Gregory's rapid departure. 'And there's one more,' he added. 'If you don't mind waiting just a bit longer...'

With his toe, he nudged the door shut—gently, this time—then turned to Kathy, folding her into his arms. 'That part—the bad part—is over, Kath,' he told her, 'laid to rest. We're starting over now.'

'A new beginning?'

'Absolutely,' he promised her. 'The very best kind, all that we didn't have eight years ago.' Gently, he kissed her, sealing his promise, then smiled down at her. 'Marry me?' he asked.

'Of course,' she began, still caught up in the dream, the words taking a moment to connect. 'But I thought we already were.'

'You didn't,' he contradicted easily. 'For the last few weeks, you've been insisting that it wasn't legal.'

'Well...' She slipped her arms around his neck, studied his expression, then asked her question—very serious now, determined to get the truth. '*Was* it?'

'Does it matter? We can still do it again,' he pointed out, an odd little quirk to his lips—not quite, but almost, a smile, 'and perhaps we'd better, after what I said to those reporters.'

'What did you say?'

'So! I didn't think you were paying attention,' he told her, the smile playing at the corners of his mouth suddenly a broad grin. 'I said that we really hadn't needed to be rescued, that we'd had plenty of food——' he paused long enough to steal a brief kiss '—and that we'd found a marvellous way to keep warm.'

'You didn't!'

'I did, and so as not to distress Father Gardiner—who's a good soul, but not the most worldly—I think it might be nice to ask him to marry us.'

'In the church?'

'As soon as it's done,' Reid promised, and kissed her again.

EPILOGUE

THE church was perfection—'Fillmore's finest design,' one expert had pronounced. The old box pews, the original pulpit and the Palladian window had been restored and were in place. The soot and the grime were gone; now the woodwork was a pristine white, the walls a soft golden yellow. Beyond the small pane windows was a springtime view—all the tender greens of trees just in leaf, the soft wash of a watercolour-blue sky.

There was no doubt about it—the church *was* perfection, but the two who had made it happen were oblivious to the beauty around them. They had eyes only for each other, were absorbed by a greater perfection—the reality of their love.

'Do you know what?' Reid murmured when the service had ended and Father Gardiner had told him that he could kiss the bride. 'They're right—all those people who say it's better the second time around.'

And it was, Kathy knew as her lips met his. It already was, and would be for the rest of their lives.

Next Month's Romances

Each month you can choose from a wide variety of romance with Mills & Boon. Below are the new titles to look out for next month, why not ask either Mills & Boon Reader Service or your Newsagent to reserve you a copy of the titles you want to buy – just tick the titles you would like and either post to Reader Service or take it to any Newsagent and ask them to order your books.

Please save me the following titles:	Please tick	√
PARADISE LOST	Robyn Donald	
SNOWFIRE	Anne Mather	
A GIRL IN A MILLION	Betty Neels	
HOUSE OF GLASS	Michelle Reid	
MASTER OF PASSION	Jacqueline Baird	
DARK SUNLIGHT	Patricia Wilson	
ECHOES OF LOVE	Jeanne Allan	
ALL IT TAKES IS LOVE	Rosemary Hammond	
SATAN'S CONTRACT	Susanne McCarthy	
TOUCHED BY DESIRE	Lynsey Stevens	
COLD FIRE	Helen Brooks	
UNWANTED LEGACY	Rachel Elliot	
DANCING WITH SHADOWS	Rosemary Badger	
HOLD BACK THE DARK	Jane Donnelly	
DRIVEN BY LOVE	Kristy McCallum	
GARDEN OF DESIRE	Laura Martin	

If you would like to order these books in addition to your regular subscription from Mills & Boon Reader Service please send £1.80 per title to: Mills & Boon Reader Service, Freepost, P.O. Box 236, Croydon, Surrey, CR9 9EL, quote your Subscriber No:................................ (If applicable) and complete the name and address details below. Alternatively, these books are available from many local Newsagents including W.H.Smith, J.Menzies, Martins and other paperback stockists from 11th June 1993.

Name:..

Address:...

....Post Code:.........................

To Retailer: If you would like to stock M&B books please contact your regular book/magazine wholesaler for details.

You may be mailed with offers from other reputable companies as a result of this application. If you would rather not take advantage of these opportunities please tick box ☐